One Perfect
Gift

One Perfect
Gift

Kathleen Morgan

Steeple
Hill®

Published by Steeple Hill Books™

STEEPLE HILL BOOKS

Steeple
Hill®

Recycling programs
for this product may
not exist in your area.

ISBN-13: 978-0-373-78661-9

ONE PERFECT GIFT

Steeple Hill Books/September 2009

First published by Revell, a division of Baker Publishing Group, in 2008.

Copyright © 2008 by Kathleen Morgan

www.SteepleHill.com

Printed in U.S.A.

For my granddaughter,
Madison Kathleen

Forgive and ye shall be forgiven.

—*Luke 6:37* KJV

Chapter One

The Plains East of Colorado Springs, Colorado
November 1933

Grand View, Colorado, wasn't quite what she expected, though she couldn't really say exactly what she *had* expected. But then, after the bustling chaos of densely populated Baltimore, this bucolic hamlet situated on the rolling plains outside Colorado Springs would be a shock to anyone's senses. Well, anyone who had grown up in a big city and rarely ventured outside it.

As the Colorado and Southern Railroad train slowed as it neared the train depot, Jessica

Ashmore gripped the rim of the window she had pulled down and, her heart thudding in her chest, stared at the approaching platform. What had heretofore seemed an exciting, adventure-laden solution to her problems had suddenly taken a decided nosedive. Perhaps her mother-in-law *had* been correct in calling her a spoiled, unrealistic fool. At the very least, the unrealistic part of the accusation rose now to confirm the older woman's perpetually unkind pronouncements.

A stiff, frigid breeze gusted past her, insolently shoving its way into the passenger compartment. Jessie shivered, leaned back, and tugged the window back up to close it. Winter must come early in these parts, she thought as she once again took her seat, noting the frost-shriveled grasses and snowcapped Pikes Peak in the distance. But then, it *was* already November first. Thanksgiving would be upon them in but another three and a half weeks.

Thanksgiving…Christmas…Jessie only hoped this holiday season could finally be celebrated like old times. A golden brown, succulent turkey on the table. Gifts for Emma. A Christmas tree glittering with tinsel and ornaments.

With a sigh, she glanced down beside her. Curled up in a bed made from her mother's threadbare wool coat, the six-year-old slept on, blissfully oblivious to the earlier cold blast of air or the train's lurching movements as it finally came to a halt at the station. The child had spent a restless night on the hard seat, and Jessie was loathe to awaken her. Nonetheless, it had to be done.

As the other passengers climbed to their feet, pulled down traveling bags, and headed off the train, Jessie bent, grasped Emma by the shoulder, and gently shook her. True to form, the girl blearily opened her bright blue eyes but an instant. Then, with a moan, she closed them and turned away, promptly falling back to sleep.

With a long-suffering shake of her head, Jessie slid her hands beneath her daughter's shoulders and legs, hauling the child to a sitting position on her lap. "Wake up, sleepyhead. We're here and it's time to get off the train."

Emma yawned hugely. Hunching her shoulders, she stiffly stretched out her arms at her sides. "We're here?" She yawned again, rubbed her eyes, then looked around. "At our new home?"

"Yes." It would be a long while—if ever—before Jessie would call this desolate spot in the middle of nowhere home. Still, for her daughter's sake, because there was nothing left for them in Baltimore anymore, she would make the effort.

Just then, the locomotive belched out a final, sibilant burst of steam. The little girl's eyes widened. "M-Mama?"

Jessie laughed. "Sounds just like a big, grumpy old dragon, doesn't it?"

"I guess so," Emma replied slowly. She cocked her head then, with a resolute nod, climbed from her mother's lap and moved to stand in the now empty aisle. "Maybe we'd better get off. Before Old Grumpy decides to fly away with us."

"And carry us off to his secret lair, filled with treasure chests full of gold and jewels, forever to make us his slaves?"

Emma grinned. "Yeah. Slaves forever."

"'Yes, ma'am,' not , 'yeah,'" Jessie automatically corrected as she stood. "Just because we're now in the Wild West is no reason to forget our manners. Remember what your grandmother always said? If you treat others with respect, you get it back in return?"

"Yes, ma'am," the girl said with a sigh, hanging her head.

Where that recollection of Louise Ashmore's frequent reminders for her only grandchild to always act the proper little lady came from, Jessie didn't know. At the realization that she, too, had inadvertently assimilated some of her mother-in-law's sayings—however right and true this particular one was—she grimaced. If Louise had ever said anything that wasn't ultimately meant to place her far above the unwashed masses, Jessie honestly couldn't recall it. But then, to be fair, she and Louise had never hit it off, not even in the early years of Jessie's marriage to Paul. And Emma's grandmother *had* always doted on her…and even more so after her son's death.

"Well, no harm's done, I suppose," Jessie said, crooking her daughter beneath her chin and lifting her troubled gaze to hers. "In fact, now that we're here in the Wild West, we'll both have to mind our manners or we're sure to lose them. I hear they use a lot of 'I reckon' and 'Yup' out in these parts."

"Really?" Delight shone in the little girl's eyes. "Is yup the Western way of saying yes then?"

"Hardly." Jessie pulled down the two black satchels and handed the smaller one to Emma. "Well, not for us to use that way anyway." She motioned down the aisle in the direction of the door where the last passenger had just exited. "Let's get going, shall we? This train's got other stops to make, and it isn't going to wait around for us."

Emma needed no further urging. Her little bag clasped firmly, she wheeled about and scampered down the aisle. Jessie was quick to follow, fearing her daughter might try to climb from the train all on her own. Fortunately, the porter was already there. Soon, both were safely assisted onto the depot platform.

"Could you tell me the way to Dr. Elizabeth Starr's office?" Jessie asked, noting that her big, scuffed steamer trunk had been unloaded and carried over to sit beside the train depot office. "We're new here and—"

"I'm afraid I wouldn't be of much help, ma'am," the porter was quick to interrupt her. "I'm not from these parts either." He lifted a hand in the direction of the depot office. "Howard Rowles will know, though. Just ask him."

Her glance strayed to the simple wooden

building with the large, bowfront windows. Through the glass panes, she could see a short, heavyset man with barely five strands of gray hair left on his balding pate bent over some paperwork at his desk. A fat, black, potbellied stove in the far corner, if the smoke spiraling from the roof flue were any indication, promised a warm fire.

"Thank you kindly." Jessie took her daughter's hand and set out for the depot office.

A bell tinkled as they walked inside. A most welcome blast of heated air engulfed Jessie as she shut the door behind her. Beside her, Emma stomped her feet and clapped her hands.

"Goodness, Mama, but it was sure cold outside!"

Howard looked up and smiled. "That it is, little missy." As he stood, his pale blue gaze met Jessie's. "And what can I be doing for you two fine ladies?"

"I was told you might be able to give me directions to Dr. Elizabeth Starr's office." Jessie walked over and extended her hand. "I'm Jessica Ashmore, Dr. Starr's new nurse."

"Are you now?" He took her hand, squeezed it gently, then released it. "Gladys changed her mind again, did she?" Howard rolled his eyes. "Holy Moses! I'm not one for sticking my nose in other folks' business, but that woman sure needs to settle on a plan and keep to it."

Unease rippled through Jessie. "Well, all I know is Dr. Starr and I have been in correspondence for some time now, and she paid our fare out here. So I take that to mean I've got a job waiting for me."

"I'd take it the same way myself, ma'am." He motioned her over to a window on the other side of the room. "Just cross the tracks using that little path over there," he then said, pointing, "then head past the street that runs parallel to the tracks until you get to the big street. That's Main Street and, being as how it's the only big street in town running north and south, you'll easily find Gates Mercantile on the corner. Take a left at the mercantile and head down Main Street. You can't miss the doc's office. The town hasn't grown all that big over the years."

She nodded. "No, I don't suppose finding anything in a town with only one main street can be all that hard. Especially not after getting around just fine for all those years in a city as big as Baltimore."

Howard whistled long and low. "Baltimore, you say? Been there once, to visit my great-aunt Mabel. Thought I'd never find my way out of that place alive."

Jessie grinned. "It can be a bit intimidating, I suppose. Especially when you're used to wide open spaces."

"And when you're not, I'll bet a place like this looks too wide and open. Too empty maybe?"

"Yes, it does." Her smile faded. "But I expect I'll get used to it." She turned to Emma, who had come over to join her, and held out her hand. "Well, best we be on our way. Once we meet with Dr. Starr, we still have to find some lodging."

"And something to eat too, Mama," her daughter piped up, taking her hand. "That bread and cheese sandwich for breakfast is long gone."

"I'm sure it is," Jessie replied, grateful that she'd even *had* a sandwich left to feed her daughter for breakfast. It had been purchased on the train last night with the last remaining money she possessed. "Just as soon as we're done meeting Dr. Starr, we'll look for some-place to eat lunch. Okay?"

Emma bobbed her head in agreement. "Okay, Mama."

As much as she hated to do so, Jessie knew she would have to ask her new employer for an additional advance on her first paycheck. It wasn't the best way to begin a new job, but it couldn't be helped. Just after she had written back to Dr. Starr, accepting the position, some unexpected bills had arrived. Bills her mother, may she rest in peace, had been unable to pay as her consumption had worsened and she had finally been let off from her job cleaning several banks near where they had lived. By the time Jessie, who was only able to procure occasional private duty nursing jobs, had settled those debts and paid her last month's rent, she'd had barely enough money to purchase food on the trip out to Colorado.

No, it couldn't be helped, she thought grimly as she made arrangements to leave her steamer trunk safely inside the station office until someone could come for it, and bade Mr. Rowles good day. It couldn't be helped, but it rankled nonetheless. Despite Louise Ashmore's subtle, and less than subtle, insinuations, she wasn't and never had been a gold digger.

Though Jessie hadn't come from old money like her late husband had, her family had been well-to-do, her father a prosperous banker, her mother the daughter of a doctor. She had been enrolled in university when she had met the dashing, dark-haired prelaw student who had wooed and won her heart during a whirlwind courtship. But her future mother-in-law hadn't seen it that way. From the start, she had done everything in her power to put an end to their relationship. And, when Jessie's father had died early into their courtship, and it had been discovered that his secret, long-standing gambling debt had wiped out all the family savings, Louise had only redoubled her efforts.

Paul had been adamant, however. No matter what, he would have the woman of his dreams. They had eloped, and there had been nothing Louise could do about it after that. Or so Jessie had thought.

But none of that mattered anymore, she reminded herself as she gripped her daughter's hand and headed from the train depot. Nothing mattered anymore but starting over, surviving. For Emma's sake, if not for her own, Jessie would do whatever it would take.

The trek across the train tracks running along both sides of the depot, and then down a cross street that intersected with Main Street, took only five minutes. Pausing next to look both directions, Jessie easily picked out Gates Mercantile. To the left and across and down several storefronts that included the newspaper office, meat market, pool hall, and another grocery store was a shingle hanging from a black, ornately turned iron. Painted on the whitewashed shingle in careful, block-style letters was "Dr. Elizabeth Starr, MD."

"There it is, sweetheart," Jessie said as she pointed down the street. "There's the doctor's office where I'll be working."

Emma glanced briefly in the direction of her mother's hand and nodded. Her attention then immediately riveted back to the mercantile beside which they were standing. In one of the windows, a colorful display of boxed games, dolls, and metal toy trucks and other cars were artfully arranged.

Jessie frowned. It was a bit early for the Christmas shopping season, but she knew the exact moment that thought crossed her daughter's mind.

The little girl looked up. "Do you think I might have a doll for Christmas, Mama? Do you think we'll have enough money to afford a real Christmas this year?"

"We'll see, sweetheart." Jessie managed a taut smile. "We'll see."

With that, she tugged on Emma's hand. They turned down Main Street and headed straight to Dr. Starr's office. A bell over the door tinkled as they walked into a small waiting room. The room was simply furnished with about six wooden chairs—three of which were occupied with what were likely patients—and a potbellied stove in one corner, with a window on either side, that more than amply heated the area. Across from the front door at the end of the room was a big desk, with two filing cabinets beside it, flanked by a long hallway.

A brown-haired, middle-aged woman with gold-rimmed glasses glanced up as Jessie closed the door behind them. "May I help you?"

Jessie indicated that Emma take one of the empty seats, then turned back to the woman. "Yes," she said as she walked over to stand before her. "My name's Jessica Ashmore and I'm to be

Dr. Starr's new nurse. We've just arrived in town. Before I seek lodging, I was wondering if it'd be possible to have a moment of Dr. Starr's time?"

The woman's eyes grew wide, and for a long moment she didn't say a word. Finally, she nodded, scraped back her chair, and stood.

"My name's Edith Baldwin. I'm Dr. Starr's receptionist and filing clerk." She held out her hand, which Jessie accepted for a quick shake. "Why don't you have a seat while I check with Dr. Starr? She's seeing a patient right now, but I'm certain she'll want to speak with you just as soon as she's finished."

Jessie smiled. "That'll be fine."

As the other woman hurried down the hallway and knocked on one of the doors, Jessie walked back and took a seat beside her daughter. The other three occupants of the room eyed her with undisguised curiosity. She smiled at them before turning her attention to her daughter.

"It won't be much longer, sweetheart, and we'll go and find ourselves something to eat. Okay?"

Emma nodded, swinging her legs back and forth from her perch on the chair. "Okay, Mama."

A few minutes later, after a whispered consultation with someone on the other side of the opened hallway door, Edith turned and headed back down the hallway. "Dr. Starr said she'd see you just as soon as she's finished with her patient," she said, finally drawing up before Jessie and Emma. "In the meanwhile, she asked that you and your daughter be shown to her office."

Picking up her traveling bag once more, Jessie stood. They followed the receptionist down to the end of the hallway and were ushered into a large, comfortable office, bright with the early afternoon sun streaming in from the big window behind the desk. Another potbellied stove stood in a far corner, radiating a most pleasant warmth. An unlit oil lamp stood on one corner of the chart- and paper-strewn desk, and Jessie was suddenly struck by the realization that this little town out in the middle of the high plains didn't yet possess electricity.

Her mouth quirked. In more ways than one, they really *were* in the Wild West.

She and Emma took possession of the two upholstered wing chairs over in the corner beside a bookcase stuffed full of medical books and journals. Her gaze skimmed some of the titles. *Merck Manual…Gray's Anatomy…Dorland's Illustrated Medical Dictionary…Textbook of Internal Medicine*. There were also several books on surgery, diseases of children and women, and even one on nutrition.

Jessie smiled. In her experience, she hadn't found a lot of physicians who evidenced much interest in nutrition and its decided impact on health. But then, her old nursing school superintendent, Elsie Lawler, had been quick to assure her that Dr. Starr was exceptional in so very many ways. Indeed, that glowing personal recommendation of a doctor she had never met had been one of the primary reasons Jessie had dared risk traipsing all the way out to Colorado to begin a new life. That, and all the others, she thought with a wry grin, like the chance at steady employment, a roof over their heads, and money for food, clothing, and even the occasional toy for Emma.

The door behind her opened just then. Jessie stood and turned. A woman of medium height with bright brown eyes, chin length, fashionably wavy black hair threaded with silver, and dressed in a navy wool skirt that fell to her calves, a white blouse, and a long white doctor's coat walked in. She shoved the stethoscope she carried into her coat pocket, then closed the door and turned.

"I'm so glad you and your daughter have arrived, Mrs. Ashmore," Dr. Starr said as she walked over and extended her hand in greeting. "Hopefully, your journey here was reasonably pleasant?"

"Pleasant enough," Jessie replied as she took the other woman's hand and shook it. "We're both glad, though, to finally be here." She glanced down at Emma. "Aren't we, sweetheart?"

The little girl nodded. "Yes, Mama." She paused, eyeing the rubber stethoscope tubing poking from Dr. Starr's pocket. "Can I listen with that sometime? I know how, you know. Mama showed me."

Elizabeth Starr smiled. "Of course you can. Probably not today, though." Her smile faded as she met Jessie's gaze once more. "There's been a complication to our plans." She paused. "Since you're here, I can only assume you didn't get my last message. The one I called and asked Elsie to deliver to you, since you didn't have a telephone."

"I last spoke with Elsie four days ago. We left our flat early the next morning to spend a day visiting Emma's grandmother before catching the train the following day. So, if you called Elsie after that…"

"Well, one way or another, it couldn't be helped." The older woman sighed. "My nurse, Gladys Pierce, the one who was resigning to get married…well, her engagement fell through. Three days ago, she came to me in tears, begging me to let her keep her job…"

Chapter Two

As the final words fell from Dr. Starr's lips, slamming the door shut on all her hopes for a fresh start, Jessie felt the blood drain from her face and the room begin to spin. She glanced wildly around and found what she was looking for—a chair.

"Excuse me," she mumbled as she stumbled over, groping for the arm of the chair. "I…I think I need to sit down."

"Yes, you most certainly do." Moving immediately to her side, Elizabeth Starr grasped her firmly around the waist and helped her take a seat. "Bend over," she then said, pushing Jessie's head down. "You know what to do. Head between your knees."

It took a minute or so before Jessie began to feel better. Finally, though, she straightened.

"I'm sorry." Her wan smile was apologetic as she met the other woman's concerned gaze. "I'm not usually given to fainting spells. I just haven't eaten since yesterday evening, and the news…the news that we've come all this way and now I don't have a job is a bit unsettling."

Elizabeth smiled in turn. "Just a bit, I'm sure." She pulled over the other chair and sat. "I'm sorry. Money's tight these days, but I'll find some way to scrape together the funds to pay for you and your daughter to return to Baltimore. It's the very least I can do."

Emma sidled over. Jessie took her hand, gripped it tightly, and gave her a reassuring smile.

"I appreciate that, Dr. Starr," she then said, again meeting the other woman's gaze. "Truthfully, though, there's nothing left for us back in Baltimore. No work, no family who we'd care to live with, and"—she swallowed her pride and, flushing hotly, uttered the final, most shameful admission—"we're out of money."

The black-haired woman frowned. "Well, then it seems you're both here to stay. We've a spare room at the rectory and a couple of extra chairs at our dinner table. I can make some calls to Colorado Springs, to the hospitals and several doctors' offices. It may take a few days, but perhaps there's work for you there."

"I'm sorry to be a burden," Jessie said. "Once I find other work, I'll pay you back for everything. And if there are no jobs available for a trained nurse, I'll gladly take whatever work is available. I'm a passably good cook, know how to clean a house, and—"

Dr. Starr gasped and held up her hand. "I've got the most wonderful idea," she exclaimed, excitement now threading her voice. "Oh, why didn't I think of this to begin with?"

She leaned over, her forearms coming to rest on her thighs. "It's good, honest work, will make use of your nursing skills, as well as your cooking and cleaning abilities, and is so very desperately needed right now. It may just cover room and board for you and your daughter, but until we can find you a paying nursing job, it's nigh unto perfect for all concerned."

At this point, Jessie was getting pretty desperate herself. And it wasn't as if she hadn't put a lot of trust in Dr. Elizabeth Starr's integrity, in just agreeing to disrupt her whole life—however glum and futile it had begun to appear—to come all the way out here. She supposed she could risk one more act of trust.

"I'm willing to take any kind of honorable work," she replied carefully. "And right about now, even just room and board in a decent place sounds pretty good. Until a paying nursing job can be found, of course."

"Oh, it's honorable work and a decent place," the older woman said with a laugh. "It's my parents' home on a ranch about five miles west of here." She paused, her smile fading. "My mother—well, actually my stepmother, but she's pretty much the only mother I ever knew—had a stroke about two weeks ago. Thank the dear Lord, though, considering all the possible consequences, she hasn't suffered severe damage. She has left-sided muscle weakness and sensory deficit, but I'm hopeful in time she'll be able to regain some use of her arm and leg. She understands whatever we say but continues to have problems with her speech. And she has to be fed with great care due to swallowing problems."

"But it could've been far worse," Jessie finished for her.

Elizabeth nodded. "Yes, it could've been far, far worse." She cocked her head. "Have you had much experience with stroke patients?"

"Yes, as a matter of fact, I have. One of my last private-duty patients had a stroke. A much worse one that eventually led to his death. I cared for him, though, for almost three months."

"Well, then it seems as if the Lord was preparing you for this."

Jessie smiled wanly. "Yes, perhaps He was."

The older woman walked back to her desk. "Do I take that to mean you're willing to accept this job then?"

As if there's really any other choice, Jessie thought. "I'm willing. What's your mother's name, by the way?"

"Abigail MacKay. She likes to be called Abby, though. And my father's name is Conor." Her hand moved to the telephone on her desk. "I'll call my father right now and make arrangements for someone to come and get you and your daughter."

In less than five minutes' time Dr. Starr had

contacted her father and offered Jessie's assistance, assistance that was, Jessie could tell from even the one-sided conversation, promptly accepted. There was a mention of someone named Sean, who would be sent to fetch them, and then the phone call was over.

"It's all set up," Elizabeth said as she hung the black, Bakelite handset back in its cradle. "My younger brother, Sean, will be here in about an hour."

She opened her desk drawer and pulled out a small coin purse. "Here's a few dollars," she said, handing over the crisp bills. "There's a café two doors down the street on your right. If you hurry, you can have that lunch I'm betting you both haven't had yet, before Sean gets here."

An impulse to refuse the money swept through her, but Jessie quashed it almost as fast as it appeared. Emma's welfare notwithstanding, she needed the sustenance just as badly. A total change in plans was enough to unsettle anyone. Some food in her belly could only help.

"I can't say when I'll have the funds to pay you back," she said as she accepted the money. "But I will. I promise."

"You don't owe me anything." The doctor smiled. "It's part of the room and board that starts right now."

"Thank you." There wasn't much more to be said after that, so Jessie turned to her daughter. "Ready for lunch, sweetheart?"

Emma disengaged herself from her mother's clasp. "I sure am, Mama. I'm starved!"

At that childish candor, both women laughed. Elizabeth gestured to their bags. "Leave them here. When Sean arrives, I'll have him load them up." She paused. "Did you have any other luggage?"

"Just a steamer trunk that we left at the depot."

"Sean can pick that up once he comes for you. Be back here in an hour. If my brother shows up sooner than that, he can easily find you at the café."

"What will he look like? So I don't end up wandering off with someone else by accident."

Dr. Starr chuckled. "Well, he's tall, with brown eyes that'll pierce clear through you, and a perpetually unruly head of black hair. He's also, if I do say so myself, a very handsome man. And he'll be dressed in Levis, some scuffed old boots, probably a canvas jacket, and wearing a black Stetson. You know," she added with a grin, "just like all the other men around."

"A real cowboy then." Jessie couldn't help but smile.

"Yep. You betcha. A real cowboy."

His hands clenched knuckle-white on the steering wheel, Sean MacKay sped down the rutted dirt road toward town. He was mad. Seething with fury mad. And neither his father nor his sister seemed to care.

What fool scheme had Beth come up with this time, to try and pawn that woman and her child off on them? Though things hadn't turned out as planned, it wasn't right of Beth now to try to ease her conscience—and responsibility—by seeking to saddle them with the care and feeding of two more mouths. And his father *knew* how he felt about strangers at the ranch. It was bad enough to have to put up with the cold-eyed glares and whispered comments every time Sean was forced to go to town.

He ground his teeth in frustration. Culdee Creek was his haven, one of the few places he always felt at peace and comfortable, accepted for who he was and how his actions spoke for him, rather than how vindictive and gossipy folk imagined him to be. But that was surely coming to an end. Soon, some unwelcome woman would be sticking her nose into what didn't concern her. And some of what didn't concern her had to do with him.

Typical older sister, Beth had told him not to make such a big fuss. That he needed to put the past behind him, and maybe then others would be able to do the same. And that he was being selfish in not wanting help for Abby, and viewing this opportunity as the God-given blessing that it was.

Well, maybe he was being a bit selfish. He knew his father was beside himself with worry and near to exhaustion. But Sean had thought what with Claire's helping out in the house, and his assistance whenever he found a free moment from the ranch work, it had been enough to swing the tide.

Obviously, though, it hadn't. Sean could still hear the frustration and utter exhaustion in his father's voice, see the barely veiled despair in his eyes, as he had tried to convince his son of the potential value of bringing a trained nurse into the house. Even now, Sean's heart twisted at the memory. Never had he wished to cause either of his parents pain. Not now, and not because of the war, or through all the years of his failed and ultimately doomed marriage.

But neither Beth nor his father understood.

"You aren't very happy with us coming to stay, are you, Mr. MacKay?"

As he drove the battered Chevrolet farm truck down the road leading out of Grand View to parts unknown, Sean MacKay, square-jawed, with thick black brows and hair—from what Jessie could see peeking from beneath his black Stetson—and even more handsome than his sister had led her to believe, shot her a quick, sharp look. "And whatever would give you that impression, ma'am?"

She shrugged. "Well, for starters, the scowl you were barely able to hide when your sister introduced us. And then the way the muscle in that jaw of yours hasn't stopped jumping ever since we left town, combined with the death grip you have on the steering wheel. Not to mention," she added, "the fact you haven't said one word to me since we got in the truck."

He didn't look her way again, instead focusing on the road ahead as if he expected something to jump out in front of them at any minute. "Whatever I think, it doesn't much matter," he growled. "My father feels he needs your help and, face it, you and your girl currently don't have anywhere else to go. So, for the time being, you're coming to Culdee Creek."

If he thought he was going to evade the issue with that flip response, he had another thought coming. Jessie was tired, upset, and just plain irritated by his manner, not to mention his lack of hospitality. And, truth be told, though it got her in trouble at times, she wasn't one to back down when others rubbed her the wrong way. Which this Levis, scuffed black boots, and tan canvas jacket clad cowboy was currently doing in spades.

"You act as if I caused the whole problem."

Sean MacKay rolled his eyes and sighed. "You're not the sort to let things lie, are you? Well, then I'll tell it to you straight. For what it's worth, anyway."

"Please do." She turned partially to better view his face. "It's best we get things settled—clear the air, so to speak—from the start."

"I know you didn't cause the problem." Once again, he glanced briefly her way. "If anyone did, it was my sister. Still, no offense, ma'am, in spite of what Beth thinks, I don't see this as such a good idea. You and your daughter bunking with us, I mean."

"And exactly why wouldn't this be such a good idea? In your opinion, of course."

"For one," he replied, turning his attention back to the rutted dirt road, "we really don't need the extra mouths to feed. We likely have more food than most folk in Grand View, what with our summer garden, chickens and their eggs, and the cattle and pigs, but that also has to feed not only my father, mother, and myself, but my brother Evan and his family. And, for another, I'm not partial to having a bunch of strangers sticking their noses into our business—and pain—right now."

Well, this surely broke all records, she thought. *A bunch of strangers, indeed!*

"If it's any consolation, Mr. MacKay," Jessie said, keeping a tight rein on her temper, "Emma and I aren't very big eaters. And I'm a licensed nurse and your mother apparently needs nursing care. A private duty nurse isn't generally someone most people would view as a stranger sticking her nose into other people's business. Indeed, they're generally very grateful to have one, especially one whose services are being acquired by only the minimal cost of room and board."

At that moment, the truck hit a rather large rut in the road. The two front balloon tires took it reasonably well, but when the solid rubber back tires rolled into the hole then pulled out of it, the vehicle rebounded several inches in the air. Inside the tall, wood slat-lined truck bed, the steamer trunk and their two traveling bags bounced and tumbled around.

"That may well be," he replied with a most annoying smirk as he apparently noticed the shaken look on Jessie's face as she hurried to grab hold of her daughter, "but we've managed just fine without you. And I reckon we could continue to do so. We're just private folk, ma'am."

"We're, or *you're*, private folk, Mr. MacKay?" she muttered finally, after settling a totally unperturbed Emma more securely back on the bench seat between them. "I was there when your sister spoke with your father. He sure didn't seem to hesitate for long when she offered him my services."

Sean MacKay's jaw went taut. "Fine. Have it your way," he ground out at last. "We're private folk, and *I'm* more private than most. And the fact that maybe my father really does need some extra help is the only reason I didn't pitch a bigger fit when I found out you were coming. I guess I didn't realize until today how hard it's been on him, physically as well as emotionally. The fact of my mother's illness, I mean."

"I'm not the sort to meddle in other's affairs, Mr. MacKay," Jessie said, her voice softening. "In addition to being a consummate professional, I'm also the soul of discretion. I don't hold with gossip, and never have."

She sensed that—aside from the obvious strain the entire family had been under since Abby MacKay's stroke—there were some additional personal issues prompting her son's reaction to Jessie and Emma's imminent arrival. One way or another, she realized rather belatedly, this was one of those times to tread lightly and back off quickly.

Emma leaned forward just then. "This is a swell truck, mister," she said, angling her head to stare up at their now grumpy-looking companion. "Could you teach me to drive it?"

Like sun on snow, the black-haired man's truculent mood melted. His lips twitched at the corners in something Jessie could almost imagine was the ghost of a smile.

"You've got a lot of growing to do, young miss," he said, glancing down at Emma, "before your feet would even touch the gas pedal. And I'm betting you won't be around here when that time finally comes."

"Then how about riding horses?" Never taking her eyes off him, she leaned back. "You do have horses, don't you? And you do know how to ride? Right?"

A chuckle vibrated from the depths of Sean MacKay's broad chest. "Yup, I know how to ride. And of course we have horses. How else do you suppose we handle all our cattle?"

Emma shrugged. "I don't know. Maybe chase them around with this truck?"

"Yeah, now that's a thought. Especially in the snow, or after a nice, long, hard rain. That's loads of fun, getting stuck up to the wheels."

"Well, maybe if you'd get your roads paved,

like we do in Baltimore," the little girl offered brightly, "you wouldn't get stuck anymore." She leaned forward again to eye him closely. "Why don't you pave your roads? Are you too poor or something?"

With a gasp, Jessie laid her hand on her daughter's shoulder and pulled her back. "That's quite enough, young lady," she said sternly. "It isn't polite to ask people such personal questions. Besides, it has nothing to do with being poor or not."

"That's right," the truck's driver offered as he shot Jessie a slanting glance. "It's got nothing to do with being poor. Quite the contrary. We actually like all the mud and bumps in the road. This is the Wild West, you know."

"Yes, I know." Emma nodded. "Mama told me all about the Wild West and the cowboys. I was hoping you'd be a cowboy, but since you drive a truck, well, now I'm not so sure."

He didn't immediately reply. Instead, he slowed the truck, then down-shifted prior to turning onto a road topped by two tall pine posts with a long wooden sign hanging from the crossbeam.

"Culdee Creek Ranch" was carved in the sign's wood, the darkly stained block letters standing out in stark contrast to the bleached color of the plank. Barbed wire, stretching for miles in both directions from either side of the pine posts, encompassed rolling fields dotted with stands of tall, densely needled pine trees. Beyond the entrance and down the hill, in a small valley flanked on the north by even more pine trees and on the south by a pond and what looked to be a stream lined with bare deciduous trees, stood a two-story wooden farmhouse.

The house, painted white and trimmed in the same shade of green as the two large, wooden barns built on high rock-and-mortar foundations, was very well kept with a long, covered front porch. Situated around the barns were corrals and various smaller pens, beside what looked to be some sort of storage building and a fenced-in chicken coop. Higher up the hill from the main house, and closer to the pines, was another smaller, wooden house, painted white but trimmed in blue.

"Well, despite your doubts, little miss," Sean MacKay finally replied as they headed down the hill toward the larger of the two houses, "I can cowboy up with the best of them. Just didn't seem the considerate thing to do, insisting you both ride back here on horses on your first day out West."

"I wouldn't have minded," Emma cried, her eyes alight with excitement. "Oooh, I do wish you would've come with horses for us to ride! Can we go riding today? Can we?"

Jessie's dismay must have been written all over her face. Sean MacKay grinned.

"Well, maybe not today, but soon, little miss." A calculating light flared in his eyes. "In fact, maybe even as soon as tomorrow. Yup,"—Sean MacKay nodded resolutely—"if the weather holds, tomorrow might be a fine time to take both you and your mother out for a nice, long horseback ride. Might as well introduce you to horses right from the start, don't you think?"

Chapter Three

A tall man who looked to be in his seventies, dressed in Levis, boots, and a red flannel shirt, awaited them on the covered front porch of the main house. White-haired with dark blue eyes and a strong blade of a nose, he stood there as if, even at his age, he was still the master of all he surveyed. Gazing at him through the rolled-up truck window as they pulled up, Jessie knew this man had to be Conor MacKay.

Beside her, his son shifted into park, pulled up on the hand brake, and turned off the engine. Without a word, he opened his door and climbed out.

"We're here, sweetheart," Jessie said to her

daughter as Sean walked around to open her door. "Now, be on your best behavior, okay?"

Emma gave a soft snort. "I'm always on my best behavior, Mama. You know that."

Which is exactly what I'm worried about, Jessie thought. Her exuberant, outgoing daughter hadn't ever met a stranger, and that sometimes led her to speak exactly what was on her mind, however blunt or tactless it might be. Though Jessie always tried to instill good manners and consideration for the feelings of others, there was only so much one could do with a six-year-old and not crush her spirit in the trying.

She smiled grimly. If there was one thing she was determined not to inflict on her daughter, it was the experience of a loveless, tightly constrained childhood such as Emma's father had endured. Still, she often walked a fine line in not overindulging Emma, and well she knew it.

"Yes, you generally do have excellent behavior," Jessie said, gripping her daughter's hand as Sean MacKay opened the truck door and frigid air spilled into the cab. "Just always stop and think of how things might sound to another. And try never, ever to hurt anyone's feelings if you can."

"A fine sentiment, ma'am," the dark-haired man said as he offered her his hand to help her down from the running board to the ground. "And does that belief apply to you as well as to your daughter?"

Jessie shot him a sidelong glance, then mustered all the courtesy she had and nodded. "Of course, Mr. MacKay. And if I gave you cause for offense during our trip here, I humbly beg your pardon." She smiled sweetly up at him, for he towered over her by nearly a foot. "So, did I?"

He didn't answer for a long moment, instead staring down at her. Finally, though, as if mentally shaking himself, he scowled. "Did you what, ma'am?"

"Give you cause for offense, Mr. MacKay?"

Before he could reply, a throat cleared loudly from the porch. Both Jessie's and Sean's gazes swung in that direction.

"So, how much longer are you two planning to keep an old man standing outside in the cold?" Conor MacKay asked with a wry grin. "Because if there's really all that more to talk about, I'll head back inside and you can join me there when you're done."

The speed with which Sean MacKay stepped back, in any other situation, would've given Jessie pause. But since she wanted just as strongly to put as much distance as she could between them, as fast as she could, the almost insulting way he immediately turned his back on her to face his father was more than fine with her. She hated, though, the flush that crept up her neck and into her face.

"Pa, this is the nurse who Beth called you about," the younger man said, making an offhand gesture in her general direction. "I'm thinking you might want to speak with her a bit, so if it's okay with you, I'll just carry her trunk up to her room." He made a move to head to the back of the truck then halted. "Er, what room would you be putting them in?"

"Beth's old room should do them fine," his father replied, a smile twitching at the corner of his mouth. "That'll situate them right next to ours, which might be more convenient in case I ever need her help during the night."

His son shrugged. "Suit yourself. It doesn't matter to me."

With that he strode to the end of the truck, slid aside the bolt, swung open the wooden tailgate, and pulled out the steamer trunk and two satchels. After walking back to wordlessly hand the satchels to Jessie, Sean next returned to heft the trunk onto his back. With his father's assistance in opening the front door, he soon disappeared into the house.

"Come on in out of the cold," Culdee Creek's owner then said, continuing to hold the door ajar. "If you haven't figured it out yet, I'm Conor MacKay. And I assume you're Jessica Ashmore. But what's your little girl's name?"

"Her name's Emma," Jessie said as she gave one satchel to her daughter, then climbed the steps to the porch. "And, please, call me Jessie. Everyone does."

"Jessie, it is, then," the tall man replied with a smile. "Welcome to our home and, please, call me Conor and my wife, Abby. Though I gather this isn't exactly the job you came all the way out here to acquire, your services are a godsend nonetheless. Just like your name means, you truly are the Lord's gift to us."

With a puzzled frown, Jessie paused inside the entry and turned back to him. "I don't understand. What has my name to do with this?"

He closed the door and moved around her.

"Jessica comes from the Hebrew word *Yiskah*, meaning, 'the Lord beholds' or 'the Lord's gift.' Of the two—and considering the circumstances— I prefer the second meaning."

"Well…thank you. I think." She blushed yet again. "I'll try my best to live up to that."

"And I've no doubt that you will." Conor indicated the room off to their right. "Put down those bags, give me your coats, and come on in and sit down. My daughter-in-law is even now making us a pot of tea to go with some freshly baked cookies." He paused to grin at Emma. "And, for you, there'll be a glass of milk to go with those cookies. How does that sound, young lady?"

Emma shot her mother a careful look, then nodded. "That sounds great, mister. I love cookies."

"Good." He took first Jessie's coat, then Emma's as her mother unbuttoned and removed it from her. "Be sure to eat as many as you want, or Claire's feelings will be hurt."

Almost as if on cue, a woman with lightly silver-streaked auburn hair and a tray laden with a porcelain teapot, cups, a glass of milk, and a plate stacked high with what looked to be oatmeal and raisin cookies walked into the living room. She smiled as she caught Jessie's eye but, as she noticed Emma, her smile widened into a grin.

"Och, ye didn't tell me the lass was so wee, Conor," she said. "If I'd known, I could've called my Sarah to send over her two girls' storybooks and old dolls."

"There'll be time enough for all that," her father-in-law said with a chuckle. "I'm hoping Jessie and her daughter will stay on with us for a while."

Though the sense of welcome and instant acceptance was heartwarming if a bit disorienting, Jessie thought it best to clear up any misunderstanding from the start. "I'll be glad to do all I can to help you with your wife," she began carefully, "but I must also tell you I'll be looking for immediate employment in Colorado Springs. Dr. Starr assured me she'd start making calls in that regard today. Not that I want you to imagine me ungrateful for your hospitality, but the sooner I can acquire some permanent nursing position…"

Conor held up a hand and nodded. "I understand this is only a temporary fork in the road for you, and totally due to unforeseen circumstances. However long you can stay, we're grateful." He looked to the woman standing there, still holding the tray. "It'll give Claire a respite from all the work of trying to manage two households, and some extra time with her husband, my oldest son, Evan. Not to mention any nursing assistance you can give my wife to help her further in her recovery."

"I'll be happy, for however long we stay, to do whatever I can for you and your wife." Jessie smiled, relieved that any potential false impressions had been so quickly and easily cleared up. "And that includes taking over the cooking and housework too." She looked to Claire. "Of course, I'll need a bit of instruction on how things run here. Like how to use all the appliances and such."

Claire chuckled. "Aye, that ye will indeed. We don't have electricity out here, ye know, or indoor plumbing, save for the hand pump in the kitchen. So the kitchen appliances are minimal, and include an icebox and a big, black, cast-iron cookstove named Old Bess."

She paused to exchange an amused glance with Conor. "And believe me, Old Bess is more appliance all by herself than most folk could ever want to handle."

* * *

As they had their tea and cookies, Conor explained the extent of his wife's limitations and needs in more detail than his physician daughter had. By the time he was done, Jessie had a pretty clear picture of Abby MacKay's nursing requirements and was already formulating a plan of care. Claire hurried to inform her that Abby came first. Only when Jessie felt she had that task under control would they next turn to the upkeep of the house.

"A few more days, one way or another, isn't any burden to me," the other woman assured her. "It's only Evan and me, now that our youngest, Jacob, has gone and taken himself a bride. And, leastwise for the time being, they've moved to Ft. Collins to be close to the agricultural college there while Jacob works on his degree. So, in spite of Evan's grousing that I spend more time here than at home these days, we'll manage just fine for a while longer."

At the older woman's generosity, gratitude swelled in Jessie. "I'll first need to meet Mrs. MacKay and examine her," she said, smiling, "but if what Mr. MacKay says is accurate, I don't anticipate requiring more than a day to get her care organized and a schedule set. Then I'll be most happy to confer with you about the house."

Conor climbed to his feet. "Well, it's only a couple of hours until supper. Claire, why don't you show Mrs. Ashmore and her daughter to their room and help her unpack their things and freshen up? I can stay with Abby and see to her care. Then, after supper, we can introduce Abby to her new nurse."

Jessie glanced up at Culdee Creek's owner. "I don't mind meeting your wife now. She's far more important than a bit of unpacking, and believe me, we didn't bring all that much. Most of what's in the steamer trunk are books and a few of Emma's clothes and toys. Well, and my uniforms and caps."

A warm light flared in the ranch owner's eyes. "Okay. Claire can take Emma to your room while we spend a few minutes with Abby. But just a few to introduce you. There's time enough for a more thorough explanation of her care after supper."

"I'd very much appreciate that." Jessie rose. "Once I've met my patient, it's so much easier to set my mind at rest. Plus, it gives me time to mull over things, the best way to care for her, I mean."

He nodded. "So, is that okay with you, young lady?" Conor then asked, looking to Emma. "May we steal your mother for about ten minutes or so?"

"Sure, mister." The little girl paused, then cocked her head. "Can I take a few cookies with me upstairs? They're *so* yummy!"

"Emma!" Jessie couldn't contain a small gasp. "That's not polite. Please apologize."

"No, no. It's fine, really it is." Conor MacKay smiled and shook his head at Jessie, then turned his attention back to Emma. "Of course you can. We don't have a lot of children around here anymore, so most of the time too many cookies go uneaten. You're really doing us a big favor, you know. Times being what they are, it wouldn't do to waste any food."

"Thanks, mister."

As Jessie watched, her daughter picked up a cloth napkin and filled it with a goodly handful of cookies. Claire then escorted her to where a flight of stairs off the main entry area led to what was evidently the second floor. Jessie watched until they were out of sight before, with a rueful sigh and shake of her head, she looked back to her host.

"That's very kind of you," she said. "She

doesn't usually get a lot of sweets. Our money only stretched so far…"

"Money's tight everywhere these days, but an occasional extravagance to make a little girl feel welcome is money well spent." He indicated the direction in which Claire and Emma had just headed. "Shall we?"

"Yes. Let's." Together, they crossed the room, entered the hall, and climbed the stairs.

Though the house was plainly furnished, it seemed to lack for no essentials, Jessie thought as they moved along. The parlor had included an upholstered sofa in a navy, green, and white plaid, two arm chairs in navy, and a wooden rocker with green chair pads, besides a book-filled, glass-fronted bookcase and several end tables adorned with oil lamps. The floor was hardwood pine covered by a large rug of worsted wool. There was also a cast-iron stove sitting on the hearth before a fireplace that Jessie surmised had given over its heating duties to the far more efficient stove. Nearby was a built-in box to hold firewood, which was filled with split pine logs.

There were rug pads on the wooden stairs leading to the second floor, which opened to a long, wide hallway with windows adorned with airy, white lace curtains on either end. She counted six doors, three on each side of the hallway. A long runner of woven shades of maroon, green, blue, and white commanded the length of the hallway floor, and the walls were adorned with myriad family photos. As they made their way down to the far end of the hall, Jessie caught glimpses of people in clothing that likely dated back to the mid 1800s all the way until today.

Conor paused at the last door on the right. "Let me go in first and tell Abby that you're here. Then I'll call you."

"That's fine," she said.

He opened the door then and walked inside, leaving it ajar. From her vantage in the hall, Jessie could see the golden glow of an oil lamp and the foot of a simply carved wooden bed. The floor was also of pine, partially covered by an oval, braided rug. Like the rest of the house she had seen so far, the room appeared spotless.

She could hear the deep murmur of Conor MacKay's voice, pitched low but filled with warmth, filled with love. At the sound, her stomach clenched. Once, she had dreamt of living to old age with Paul at her side, content, comfortable, and loved. But that was never to be. Indeed, that dream had died long before his untimely death. He had never been the man she had imagined him to be.

"Mrs. Ashmore," her host called softly of a sudden. "You can come in now."

Jessie wrenched her attention back to the moment at hand. What might have been no longer mattered. The present held enough challenges to occupy her. And the present was reality, even if it might never be the stuff of dreams.

But then, dreams were but illusions. She had a daughter to feed and clothe, and a living to make. She couldn't afford to squander any more time—or misguided hopes—on useless and ultimately futile dreams.

Chapter Four

Jessie had met and cared for many stroke patients, but from the first moment she laid eyes on Abby MacKay, she knew this patient was different. There was none of the frustrated agitation or air of hopelessness in this woman's demeanor. Her gaze, as she met Jessie's, was bright and inquisitive but overlaid with a peaceful calm. Though the left side of her mouth drooped and it was evident from the slight cant of her body in the same direction that some lasting damage had been done, the right side of her mouth lifted in what could only be construed as a welcoming smile.

After squaring her shoulders and returning the

other woman's smile, Jessie walked into the room and over to stand before her. She squatted beside the upholstered wing chair padded with pillows to help support Abby, and took up her hand.

"My name's Jessie," she said, "and it seems that the good Lord has sent me to be your nurse. I hope that's all right with you."

The woman, who looked to be in her sixties, slowly nodded her silvered head. "G-God's will…is m-my will."

Though her speech was halting and slurred, Jessie was able to understand her. She nodded in turn, gave Abby's hand a gentle squeeze, then stood.

"Good." She paused to scan the other woman. Her hair was neatly combed and plaited into one long braid. She appeared well-nourished, her white nightgown was clean, and her hands and feet looked to be in normal alignment.

Someone—likely Dr. Starr—had instructed them on good skin care and prevention of contractures of the limbs. This would make Jessie's job a lot easier. The patient was in excellent condition, unlike most stroke patients she had encountered.

"Has any sort of exercise program been started with your wife?" she asked, turning to Conor.

"Just the sort to keep her limbs from stiffening."

"Then it's time to begin some more complex exercises in the hopes of helping Abby"—she glanced back to her patient—"regain some use of her left side. I'll start out very slowly and gently, but it's really the necessary next step. And that will include helping her to start walking again too."

A look of surprise, then hope, then gratitude flared in the older man's eyes. "We'd like that very much. And whenever you need help, either I or Sean will be available to assist you."

At the mention of his son's name, it was all Jessie could do to squelch a grimace. With his barely veiled hostility toward her, she doubted Sean MacKay would be of much aid. Though he might truly wish to help his mother, his negativity regarding her nurse would surely taint the air and adversely affect Jessie's state of mind. The task ahead was challenging enough without his doubtful attitude.

"Most times," she said, "we'll be able to schedule the exercise sessions to suit your routine, so likely there won't be much need to impose on your son. I'm sure he's very busy with work on the ranch."

He eyed her quizzically, then nodded. "Well, he *is* the ranch foreman and most times does have his hands pretty full, but things slow down a bit here in the winter. So, we'll keep him as a backup, just in case we need him. I'll be glad, though, to be your main assistant." Conor graced his wife with a loving look. "I cherish any and every chance I get to be with Abby."

Jessie couldn't help but note the depth of their affection for each other. It struck a bittersweet note with her. Bitter, because she had once known such happiness, and after Emma's birth, it had vanished so swiftly and permanently she almost wondered if the emotion had always been little more than an illusion. Yet sweet as well, for she was glad to see that a long-term, devoted marriage was possible. Well, for some folk anyway. She wasn't so sure *she'd* ever find it.

But that was more of Louise's negativity creeping in, Jessie was quick to remind herself. After all, her mother-in-law was halfway across the country. Indeed, for all practical purposes, halfway across the world. Even for her only grandchild, Louise would never venture far from her beloved Baltimore. For all practical purposes, Jessie was free of her once and for all.

"Well, I'll gladly take you up on your offer," she said, forcing her thoughts back to the matter at hand, "and make good and frequent use of you." Her glance strayed to Abby, who was regarding her with a piercing intensity. "The more aggressively we work with you now, Mrs. MacKay, the better the long-term outcome."

The older woman nodded. "I'm b-but clay in the p-potter's hands. A-as are w-we all. As are we a-all…"

There was something burning deep within her gaze, some additional message, Jessie realized as she returned Abigail MacKay's steady regard. It was almost as if she were trying to tell Jessie something. Something she imagined Jessie needed to know.

But what? That there was yet hope in the midst of despair? That shattered dreams might still be reconstructed into something even more beautiful and lasting?

Well, Jessie already knew that. She just didn't want to try so hard anymore. She just wanted to get by, and save the hope and dreams for her daughter. That'd be enough for her. It had to be.

"Yes, we *are* all clay," she acknowledged at last. "Some of us, though, are far more malleable, more resilient, than others."

Their bedroom was pleasant enough, Jessie thought later that evening when she had the leisure to study the room more closely. In addition to the white, enameled steel bed covered with a quilt in various shades of cheerful pastels, there was also a tall chest of drawers and a dresser topped with a mirror. Both were painted white with dainty floral decorations and neat, scrolling stripes. Near the window, hung with white, crisscross Priscilla-style curtains, stood a small wooden table, a chair, and the requisite oil lamp for early morning and evening light. To complete the cozy room, a large braided rug in coordinating shades of pink, blue, green, and white covered the floor, and several framed watercolor pictures hung on the walls.

Jessie smiled as she walked over to more closely examine the artwork. Colorful and well done, they were still obviously the product of youthful hands. Abby must have been a doting mother, and proudly hung her children's artistic undertakings on the walls. Noting these maternal touches, Jessie knew she would've liked the woman even before she had met her. And now, after meeting her in person, this room but confirmed the character of her newest patient.

All in all, it had turned out to be a surprising day. She never would've believed that, in the course of hours, she could've gone from what appeared a devastating change of plans to a sense of acceptance and ease with a family of total strangers. Well, almost all of the family, Jessie added with a wry twist of her lips. There was always Sean MacKay.

He hadn't said much to her, or to anyone, at supper. She supposed it was his way of keeping his inhospitable opinions to himself. Not that his grumpy mien had been lost on anyone at the table, if the puzzled looks and quiet scrutiny had been any indication. But there wasn't much she could do about the young foreman's attitude at any rate. Well, at least not much she cared to do.

Sean MacKay would either come to accept her or not. In the meanwhile, she had her hands full enough with her real patient, not to mention caring for Emma and continuing to look for a permanent job. If any job like that was even to be found in these parts.

A freshened wave of fear washed over her. What if…what if she couldn't find another job before this one with the MacKays ran out? With room and board her only payment for her work, there'd be no way to save any money to tide them over or buy a train ticket back to Baltimore.

Not that she ever wanted to return to Baltimore. Even more painful memories remained to haunt her there.

She sighed. She had tried so hard not to be bitter over the blows life had dealt her. She had tried to see the good in life, and in people, its blessings and its joys. Yet, especially of late, the anger and resentment hovered at the edge of her thoughts, coloring all she said, did, and believed.

There were so many times when she all but cursed her dead husband for leaving them, for his cowardice. For not being the spouse she needed, or the father their daughter deserved. For destroying her dreams of a happy, fruitful life surrounded by all their children. For, oh, *how* she had wanted many children!

And his mother…Try as she might, Jessie couldn't forgive her for her hard-heartedness, even as she knew her own unwillingness to forgive was, in its own way, equally as hard-hearted.

Perhaps worst of all, the bitterness, the resentment, the lack of mercy, had distanced her from the Lord. She still went to church, still said her nightly prayers with Emma, still even read her Bible on occasion. But Jessie knew the truth. She had let her pain build a wall around her heart, and she wouldn't let even God in anymore.

"Come on, sweetheart." With an effort, Jessie wrenched her morose thoughts back to more pleasant things. "Time for bed."

Jessie motioned for her nightgown-clad daughter, who was merrily skipping around the perimeter of the braided rug, to head toward the bed. She had already turned back the covers to expose freshly laundered, crisply ironed sheets. What with the thick down comforter that lay just beneath the quilted coverlet, she knew they'd both sleep snugly tonight. Once she had her perennially effervescent and energetic daughter finally settled down, that is.

"Don't you think this is the most beautiful

bedroom you've ever seen, Mama?" Emma asked as she skipped over to halt before her mother. "We could live here forever and not need anything more."

"Yes, it is very lovely," Jessie replied as she helped her daughter climb into bed. "And, for as long as we stay here, we'll enjoy it very much. But you do realize, don't you," she asked as she pulled up the covers and tucked them in beneath the little girl's chin, "that we're only staying here a short while? That this isn't our forever home?"

"But isn't that for God to say, Mama?" Eyes the color of a blue sky on a sunny day gazed up at her. "Preacher Thompson said God puts us where He wants us, so we can do the very best we can for Him."

Leave it to an innocent—albeit sometimes a very *precocious* innocent—to remind her of what should really matter in life. Jessie smiled, though the effort was forced and lacked much warmth.

"It most definitely is for God to say. But I seriously doubt He intends for us to stay here. This is just a temporary respite, until we really do find our forever home."

Emma snuggled deeper into the covers.

"Maybe so, Mama. But God brought us here for a reason. And Grandma Ashmore once told me that God doesn't do *anything* without a reason."

Chapter Five

"Would you like a little nap before we begin the morning exercises?" Jessie asked a week later as she fastened the last button on the loose house-dress she had put on Abby after her bath. "Or do you feel up to some more activity?"

"L-let's get them d-done," the older woman managed to slowly enunciate. "Then, m-maybe a n-nap before l-lunch."

Jessie grinned. "You're a real go-getter, Abigail MacKay. But I guess you'd have to be, what with a husband, children, and a ranch household to manage."

Abby smiled softly, the slight droop to the left side of her face making her mouth tilt upward a bit crookedly. "N-not so much th-these days. L-lucky I h-have a lot of h-help."

"You'll be running things just fine soon enough." Jessie leaned back, then took up her patient's left arm, supporting her hand and forearm. "How about we start with some wrist exercises and work our way up?"

As Abby opened her mouth to reply, someone rapped on the bedroom's doorframe. Jessie glanced over her shoulder. It was Claire.

"Beth's on the phone and would like to speak with ye," the auburn-haired woman said. "If ye're in the middle of something, I can tell her ye'll call her when ye get a free moment."

"We were just getting started with Abby's exercises." Jessie gently laid her patient's arm back on the bed. "I'm sure whatever Beth has to tell me, it'll only take a few minutes. And, knowing how busy doctors are when in clinic, if I don't talk with her now, I might not catch her again until the end of the day."

Abby nodded. "Y-you're right about th-that." She made a shooing motion with her unaffected hand. "G-get along. Talk w-with Beth. I'm not g-going anywhere."

"You say that now," Jessie replied, chuckling. "But some day soon, I'm going to turn around for a second, and you'll be heading off to who-knows-where."

To the laughter of the other two women, she turned and hurried from the room. Only a week at Culdee Creek, she thought, marveling, and already she felt at home and among the dearest of friends. She had almost always been able to develop a warm rapport with her patients, though with some far more quickly than with others. But this was different. It was almost…almost as if she had finally found the safe and loving haven she had sought all her life.

With a sharp shake of her head, Jessie firmly tossed that silly little dream aside. Without a doubt, the MacKays were kind, generous, godly people. But there was no hope of a home here. She was but an employee, and a very temporary one at that.

The house's single telephone was in the kitchen. Jessie pulled out a chair at the kitchen table and scooted it close to the wooden stand whereupon the telephone sat. Taking up the receiver, she pressed it to her ear.

"Dr. Starr? This is Jessie. Claire said you wished to speak with me."

"Yes, I did," came a woman's voice through the phone. "I'm sorry to have taken so long to get back to you about potential jobs in the Springs, but what with a crazy schedule in the clinic, plus waiting for my esteemed colleagues to return my calls…well, it's taken longer than I expected."

"I understand." Jessie's grip tightened on the receiver, and she could feel her pulse begin to quicken. "I've been keeping rather busy here as well." She paused. "Do you have any good news to report? Any physicians looking for a nurse?"

Beth sighed. "Unfortunately, no. Like most places these days, their employees are staying put where they are. And I even tried the local hospitals. Spoke with the nursing directors at Glockner Sanatorium and St. Francis and Bethel General hospitals, and none of them have any openings right now either. All of them did say to check back with them every few months, though. I gave them the ranch phone number to contact you."

Though her disappointment was acute, Jessie also knew Dr. Starr had gone out of her way to try to make up for the part she had played in this whole fiasco. And it wasn't as if she and Emma had been thrown out on the street. Far, far from it. They had a cozy, comfortable room, three square meals a day, and a warm, welcoming, and immensely grateful family who had almost, to a man, gladly taken them in.

She must have been silent too long, though. Beth Starr sighed again, deeply this time.

"I'm so sorry, Jessie," she said. "You have my word I'll keep on this until I find you a job."

Jessie forced a tight smile and began to play with the curly telephone cord. "I know. It wasn't anyone's fault. I'll just feel better when I'm finally settled in my own place, with a permanent job, that's all. A permanent nursing job."

"Maybe something will open up after the New Year," the other woman ventured hopefully. "No one likes to make changes during the holidays. And I'm certain you'll have plenty to do with my mother until then, and probably even longer. You and Emma will at least have a nice place in which to spend Christmas. We MacKays are famous for having the most wonderful Christmas celebrations. And Thanksgiving ones too, for that matter."

Thanksgiving…Jessie hadn't given that holiday much thought, considering they hadn't been able to afford to celebrate it for the past few years. But, glancing at the calendar hanging on the back of the kitchen door, she realized it was only two and a half weeks away.

If Beth's words struck anywhere near the mark, the odds were strong there might actually be the chance of a real celebration this year. For Emma's sake, Jessie had to be happy for that. And maybe, she reluctantly admitted, for her sake too.

"Well, thank you for all the phone calls you made, Dr. Starr," Jessie said, deciding it was past time to return to her patient. "I truly appreciate all your assistance with my job search."

"You're most welcome. Would you tell my mother that I'll be coming by tomorrow afternoon to pay her a visit? I'd like to—"

Something caught the edge of Jessie's vision. Momentarily distracted, she angled her head in the direction of the doorway. Sean MacKay, his arms folded across his chest, his expression hard and considering, stood there, leaning against the doorjamb. Her stomach gave a sickening lurch.

"Jessie? Are you still there?"

She jerked her attention, if not her gaze, back to the woman on the other end of the line. "Yes, Dr. Starr. I'm here. And I'll be glad to tell your mother that you'll be visiting tomorrow."

"Good. Bye for now then."

"Yes, good-bye, Dr. Starr."

He had something on his mind, Jessie knew, taking an inordinate amount of time to hang up. He had something on his mind, and she doubted any of it would be kind or gently worded.

She swallowed, squared her shoulders, and turned. "Yes, Mr. MacKay?" Jessie asked, meeting his blistering gaze. "Is there something I can do for you?"

He didn't answer straight off. Finally, though, he expelled a long, deep breath. "You can't wait to hightail it off this ranch, can you? No matter how badly my mother needs you, or how much my father is coming to depend on you?"

The censure in his accusation took Jessie aback. But only for an instant. "And exactly why would *you* care? You never wanted me here in the first place."

"Maybe I'm changing my mind."

Jessie's laugh was incredulous. "You expect me to believe that, after barely speaking more than five or six words to me in the past week? Come, come, Mr. MacKay. I'm not that easily bamboozled, you know."

He eyed her for a long moment, then let his arms fall to his sides as he straightened. "Well, it really doesn't matter anyway, does it? Whether you're easily bamboozled or not? Just like it doesn't much matter if my mind was beginning to change about you. You'll be long gone soon enough, and that'll be the best for everyone."

She walked over to stand before him. "Best for you, to be sure. But it won't be today, or tomorrow, or the next. And now, if you don't mind, would you step aside so I may pass? Your mother's waiting for me upstairs and, for as long as I *am* here, I intend to take the very best care of her that I can."

He didn't budge but continued to stand there, blocking her way. Jessie forced herself to meet his scowling gaze and choke back her sense of rising intimidation. She had faced down far more daunting patients and physicians in her nursing career. She wasn't about to let some…some simple cowboy back her down now.

"See that you do, Mrs. Ashmore," he finally said, moving out of her way.

Jessie's eyes narrowed. "Is that a threat, Mr. MacKay? Because if it is, I don't take kindly to threats."

Sean MacKay smiled, but the look never reached his eyes. "No, it's not a threat, Mrs. Ashmore. I just want the best for my mother, that's all. As hard as you might find that to believe, I just want the best for her."

"Son, a moment of your time. I think we need to talk."

Sean paused later that evening outside his parents' bedroom door, where they had just finished settling his mother in bed for the night. Somehow, he knew what the topic of the talk would be, and he wasn't in the mood right now to belabor the issue of Jessica Ashmore's presence in their home. Especially with how taken everyone else seemed to be with her and her daughter.

One glance at the expression of utter resolve in his father's eyes, however, quashed any hope of using weariness as an excuse to avoid the inevitable. Sean sighed and nodded his acquiescence.

"Fine. Where do you want to talk?"

"Downstairs for starters," his father said. "This isn't something I care to discuss outside in the hall."

"No, I suppose not. How about the kitchen?"

Conor nodded. "I'll be there in five minutes. I just want to let your mother know where I'll be."

Sean headed downstairs. Once in the kitchen, he relit the oil lamp, placed it in the middle of the table, and took a seat on one of the ladder-back chairs. The lamplight bathed the room in a golden glow and, for a moment, he was content to bask in its comforting radiance. Soon, though, the restlessness returned. He rose, walked to the icebox, and pulled out a pitcher of milk. After pouring himself a glass, he put away the pitcher and went back to his seat.

The milk was quickly consumed and the glass shoved aside. Resting both arms before him on the red-and-white-checked oilcloth, Sean contemplated his clasped hands—and the confrontation to come. How was he going to explain his muddled feelings about Jessie to his father, he wondered, when he couldn't even sort through them himself?

Their tight finances notwithstanding, it had

been bad enough when his father had announced they'd be having some live-in guests for a while, upending the carefully constructed, safe little fortress Sean had at long last been able to build about his heart after his wife Charlotte's death. Little Emma wrenched at him every time he saw her, a physical reminder of the children he had always wanted and would never have. But seeing her mother every day in some capacity or another, no matter how hard he tried to avoid her, was even worse. She was, for want of a better word, stunning.

Her honey blonde hair wasn't cropped in the current style, nor forced into what he considered unnatural waves. When it wasn't tucked up beneath her nursing cap during the day, the shining length was tied with a simple black ribbon at the back of her neck before cascading down in shimmering waves to well below her shoulder blades. Her skin was a creamy ivory, tinged with rose at her cheeks, her lips were soft and pink, and her nose was pert and charming. But it was her eyes, from the first moment he had gazed into them, that had truly been his undoing.

A dark, cobalt blue, like some jewel held up

to the sun, they seemed to change hue and quality with each blink. One moment they glinted with endless shades of indigo. In the next, they sparkled, alive with light. And then they would suddenly calm like the surface of a lake, gleaming softly with a compelling depth and emotion.

In all his life, Sean had never seen eyes like hers. They were like a magnet, inexorably drawing him to her. Drawing him to something he had finally surrendered, never to dream of or hope for again.

His hands clenched and he ground his teeth in fury. Fury at her for coming into his life just when he had finally gotten it back under control, but even more fury at himself for his weakness. At his stupidity in imagining he could ever be in control of anything, ever again.

For an exquisitely painful instant, Sean's thoughts flashed back to that horrible October day in France. The day he had watched his boyhood friend shot dead by men drawn by lot from their own army unit. Even now, after fifteen years and a war that seemed little more than a horrible memory, Sean could still smell the sweat and fear, see Carl shaking violently as they tied the blindfold over his eyes, and hear that final, fatal click of the carbines as they were cocked and then aimed at the single man standing before that ruined, ancient stone wall. Even now, the memory made Sean's heart beat faster, his throat go dry, and his hands turn damp.

Ultimately, Carl might have died because of his lifelong lack of consideration for the consequences of his actions, and his faithless, failed attempt at running from what he no longer cared to face, but how had *he*, his supposed best friend, fared much better? For his part in the tragic fiasco, Sean *had* managed to survive with his life. That, however, was the only thing left intact. He'd been betrayed by his best friend, and he struggled still to come to terms with that, to forgive. Honor, self-esteem, and the relationship with the woman he loved and had counted the days until he could return to—all were in ruin. Ruined beyond redemption, no matter how long and hard he had striven to repair them.

None of that mattered anymore. Charlotte was dead, as was her older brother, both taken from him in what seemed the blink of an eye, if in entirely different times and ways. There was no longer hope of salvaging anything of value. His life was what it was, something to be lived and endured. He would do the best he could, even as he wondered how much value even that simple aspiration really possessed anymore.

Problem was, Sean had only recently realized with Jessie Ashmore and her daughter's arrival, the best was no longer good enough. As innocent as they both might be in it all, their presence threatened the safe, circumscribed little fortress he had finally managed to throw up around himself. And it scared him. Scared him a lot.

He didn't know what would happen if those walls ever crumbled. Could he find the strength to rebuild them again? Would he even *have* the strength? No one—*no one*—realized how close to the precipice he stood, or how easily he could lose his balance and tumble into the gaping maw of despair.

There were days—and even more nights— when it was all Sean could do to cling to the fragile branch of hope. Hope for what, he no longer knew. He had lost his reputation, his honor, in the war. He had lost his best friend and the respect of his friend's family, not to mention the respect of many others hereabouts. But, worst of all, he had lost his wife's love, and likely that of God Himself, if their four dead babies were any indication.

He didn't need now, atop everything else, to shame himself in futile and ultimately self-destructive yearnings after his mother's nurse.

The footfall of booted feet on the hardwood floor leading down toward the kitchen drew Sean up short. He straightened, lifting his head to meet his father's gaze as the older man halted in the doorway. They stared at each other for a long moment before Conor walked over, pulled out a chair, and straddled it, facing his son.

"I don't know what sort of grudge you're carrying against Jessie, or why," his father began without preamble, "but don't you think it's long past time you let it go? Already, in just a week's time, she's done wonders with your mother, not to mention she's the kindest, most generous and hard-working woman I've ever met."

"Don't you think I've noticed all that?" Sean ground out, glancing down, once more, at his hands. "It's nothing personal against her. I just don't like…being around her."

"You do realize, don't you, that you're not making much sense?"

Sean lifted his head and managed a weak smile. "Yeah, I realize that."

His father studied him intently until, finally, a light of recognition dawned in his eyes. "You're attracted to her, aren't you? And you're afraid of your feelings."

"Feelings?" Sean gave a bitter laugh. "More like lust, I'd say. I haven't been with a woman since Charlotte, and considering she died two years ago and we weren't particularly close since she lost the last baby a year before that…"

"Well, be it lust or affection, your behavior toward Jessie then makes even less sense." Conor paused, cocking his head. "A man who wants a woman doesn't usually treat her as if he can't stand the sight of her. Care to explain yourself a little further?"

"After being around her just a week?" His son shrugged. "I'm not sure I've sorted it all out myself."

"But you've sorted some of it out."

Sean shot his father a disgruntled look. "Can't you give a man a little space? I feel enough of a fool without having to admit it to you."

Conor sighed. "All those years you were married to Charlotte, I bit my tongue, held back the thoughts that I wanted to speak. As did your mother. But, oh, the prayers we raised on your behalf to the Lord!" He shook his head. "Yet, when I see how long you've been cutting yourself off from life, from daring to pick yourself up and try again, and how bitter it's making you, to the point that you can't even face your emotions in an honest, healthy way…"

He reached across and clasped Sean by the shoulder. "Don't do this, son. There's a reason Jessie and her daughter were sent to us. Nothing is ever wasted or without a purpose in the hands of the Lord. And maybe, just maybe, they're as much a gift to you as they already are to us. Don't shut your heart to them, or to the chance of finally finding the love and happiness you've always deserved."

Angrily, Sean wrenched from his father's grip, slammed back his chair, and rose. "And who said this problem I'm having with Jessie Ashmore had anything to do with love, or even about God? I told you to give me some space about this, and I meant it!"

Conor gazed up at his son and said nothing. In the tension-laden silence, a soft voice unexpectedly intruded.

"Uh, please...I'm sorry to interrupt," Jessie said, shooting Conor an embarrassed glance, "but your wife is calling for you. I checked on her, and she's crying and very upset. Though it's likely just related to her stroke—the tears, I mean—I thought you might like to go to her."

Conor climbed to his feet. He gave Sean a long, measuring look, then turned to Jessie. "Yes, thank you. We were done here at any rate. And I'd indeed like to go to my wife."

With that, he wheeled about and stalked from the room. Jessie watched until he disappeared up the stairs, then looked to Sean. "Well, I guess I'll be heading back upstairs myself—"

"Wait a minute," Sean said, holding up a hand. "First, tell me something."

"Yes, and what would that be?"

"Exactly how much of our conversation did you hear," he growled, "before you finally decided to interrupt?"

Chapter Six

*D*oes just about every word that comes out of Sean MacKay's mouth have to be so blunt and offensive? Jessie wondered. It was getting to the point she wanted nothing more than to avoid him whenever she could. He was the one black spot in an otherwise extremely pleasant working and living situation.

Meeting his flinty gaze, however, as she struggled to formulate some reply that wouldn't result in yet another barrage of angry words, Jessie caught a fleeting glimpse of vulnerability—and fear. But fear of what?

She thought back to what she had overheard of the conversation between father and son, of the mention of a wife named Charlotte who apparently neither Conor nor Abby had approved of. That Sean seemed to have been so deeply wounded by his marriage he had withdrawn from life and loving. And that, somehow, some way, Jessie was tied into all of this, in some emotional context that involved Sean.

At the very least, she knew Sean didn't trust her. But why? That he might not easily trust others, especially strangers, she could understand. But what if this inability to trust went deeper? What if he somehow feared that she might wound him as his wife appeared to have done?

It didn't make a lot of sense, especially since he had taken an instant dislike to her before she could prove herself one way or another. And it was so unfair. He had gone on the offensive first thing…as if to protect himself, rejecting her before Jessie had a chance to reject him.

Compassion filled her. She understood what it was like to lose trust, to steel her heart from the blows of others. Indeed, how much different was her reaction to him when they had first met? He had quickly rubbed her the wrong way too.

"I heard enough to realize that you and your father were arguing over women in general, and me and your wife in particular," Jessie finally replied, heat creeping into her cheeks. "Your father also seemed to think you felt some attraction toward me. Personally, though, I'm guessing it's a lot more complex than that. That maybe I just represent all that you fear about women."

He glared at her with glacial anger. "I'm not afraid of women. Far from it."

"Well, that may be. Leastwise in a physical sense." Jessie wet her lips, contemplating how best to phrase what she next wanted to say. "I guess I was thinking more of personal rejection and the potential for causing you pain."

"And how would you know anything about what I might fear? You presume a lot, Mrs. Ashmore."

She shrugged. "Maybe I do. But you're kidding yourself if you imagine you're the only person here who hasn't been rejected, and hurt, and made to feel worthless. And I wasn't talking about how you've treated me since the first moment we met, either."

Surprise flickered across his face and then

some other emotion. Was it regret, shame? Jessie wasn't certain.

He did release a deep, shuddering breath, then motioned toward the table. "Maybe we should have a seat and talk this through. No matter my personal reasons for my reactions whenever I see you, I know I haven't been fair. For that, I'm sorry. None of this is your fault. Not now, and not ever."

It was the closest he had ever come to an apology, and Jessie wasn't fool enough to quibble over the finer points of etiquette. She walked over to the chair Conor had left standing askew, straightened it, then sat down.

"I'd like that very much, Mr. MacKay," she said, looking up at him. "To talk this through, if we can."

He stared at her for a long moment, then took his own seat at the table. "I'm not one for spilling my guts to everyone I meet," he finally said. "And I'm not going to do it for you, either. I don't want, or need, your pity."

My, but he's as prickly as a hedgehog, Jessie thought. *Well, go ahead and roll up into a tight little ball. At least we're finally talking.*

"I didn't come here to make your life difficult," she began softly, "and for your sake, if I could, I'd leave. But first I've got to find another job. And I'd also like very much to see your mother farther on the way to recovery before I leave." She smiled. "I'm not one for leaving any job unfinished, not to mention, I really care about your mother. And your father, and the rest of your family, for that matter."

"But not about me."

Jessie laughed. "Well, you haven't exactly made it easy to like you, much less care."

Something that sounded almost like a chuckle rumbled deep in Sean's chest. "I reckon I haven't, have I?"

"We all have our reasons." She glanced down for a second, wondering if she should share some of her own reasons for coming out here, much less if he would even care to hear them. But then, what did she have to lose? The worst that could happen is he'd know a bit more about her and still not want anything to do with her.

"The day my old nursing school superintendent contacted me about a possible job with your sister," Jessie forced herself to go on, "well, it was the first bright spot in my life after months of darkness. My mother had just died; I could barely find enough employment as a private duty nurse to sustain Emma and me financially, and I didn't know from one day to the next if our landlord would evict us. My mother-in-law was even beginning legal proceedings to take Emma away from me. Not only had I apparently failed her son in life, but she was also convinced I was an unfit mother. At the very least, after all, I could barely keep food on the table and a roof over our heads."

She smiled sadly. "Of course, it didn't matter to Louise—my mother-in-law—that we were nearly destitute because her son lost all our money in the stock market crash. I guess she was just mired so deeply in her own grief that she needed to lay blame somewhere other than at her own feet. Thankfully, for Emma's sake anyway, we were finally able to get past some of that."

He didn't say anything, just watched her, silent and thoughtful.

"Coming out here to Colorado seemed not only a way to start fresh, but also the only way to keep my daughter. Once I had that firm job offer from your sister, Louise had to let the legal proceedings go." She sighed and glanced at the ceiling before meeting his gaze once more. "Still, maybe I should've let my mother-in-law take Emma. Emma would've never lacked for anything, living with her in that big, fine house. But I wanted more for Emma than just material possessions. I wanted her to grow up knowing love, being loved. And Louise never had much of that to go around, even for her own son."

"She doesn't seem the worse for the wear, your daughter, I mean," the dark-haired man sitting across from her offered. "She's a very happy and outgoing child."

"She's certainly taken a liking to you. I hope she doesn't make a nuisance of herself."

His lips curled upward in what Jessie could almost imagine was a tender smile. "No. She doesn't make a nuisance of herself. But it doesn't matter at any rate," he said, his smile disappearing almost as fast as it had appeared. "The two of you will be gone soon enough."

"What choice do we have? It doesn't mean, though, that we can't all make the best of the time we have together. That we can't all try to be kind to each other, to be friends."

"Friends?" Sean gave a wry laugh. "I'm not one for making friends anymore."

"And why's that?" Jessie slanted him a curious look. "Because *you* can't be counted on or, rather, *they* can't be counted on?"

His eyes widened, then went dark. "Depends on who you talk to, I reckon."

"Well, I'm talking to you. Besides, I tend to make up my own mind about people. I'm kind of bullheaded about things like that."

He grinned then. "Somehow, that doesn't surprise me."

Jessie gave a soft snort. "And of course you're not a bit stubborn yourself."

"I prefer to think I just know what I like, and that I'm rarely wrong."

She considered him carefully, realizing she was about to tread on shaky ground. "But when you are wrong, you're also a big enough man to admit it."

His smile faded. "I'd like to think so. When I am wrong. I'm not ready to say, though, that I'm wrong about you. But I am willing to give it a chance. If you are too, that is."

Yes, Sean MacKay really was a prickly sort,

and not easily led or manipulated, Jessie thought. But she couldn't say she blamed him. She had never liked others trying to lead her where she didn't wish to go, either.

"I'm willing to give it a chance," she said. "And, for starters, I've got two favors to ask of you."

"Two?" His gaze narrowed. "Are you always such a greedy woman?"

"Not usually." A smile tugged at one corner of her mouth. "But since we're getting off to such a late start, I figured there was a bit of catching up to do."

"Well, don't keep me waiting. I'm not promising you anything, but I'm willing to listen."

What a careful, guarded man! Hands clasped before her, Jessie leaned forward.

"First, I'd like to move to a first-name basis, if that's all right with you."

He nodded. "That's doable, I reckon. And the second favor?"

"I'd like to learn how to ride. You did, after all, promise to take Emma and me riding."

"That was before I wanted you to stay on a while. The plan was to scare you into leaving. I even had the perfect horse for the job picked out for you."

"And now?" She cocked her head, an impish smile on her lips.

Sean laughed. "Now, I think I just might choose a gentler one for you."

Even with the kitchen door shut, Jessie heard the first guests drive up and honk their car horn the day before Thanksgiving. She finished toweling Emma's hair and quickly ran a comb through her tangled locks, then pulled both sides up from her face and fastened them at the top of her head with a tortoiseshell barrette.

"Quickly now," she then urged her daughter, handing her a hairbrush. "Finish dressing, then go to the parlor and brush out your hair before the fire until it's dry. I'll join you just as soon as I've got the kitchen put to rights and our things stored back in our room."

"Okay, Mama." Emma finished tucking her flannel shirt into her denim overall pants, then slipped her stockinged feet into her sturdy shoes. As she made a move for the door, however, Jessie stopped her.

"Wait a minute, sweetheart," she said as she stooped and began folding up the cuffs of the overlong denims—some of the old children's clothes Claire had given them—then tied her shoes. "Between pants too long and laces untied, you're sure to trip and fall on your face before you're halfway across the hall."

"Oh, Mama!" Emma rolled her eyes in girlish exasperation. "I was going to fix all that once I got to the parlor. I'm not *that* clumsy."

Jessie stood and patted her cheek. "I know, sweetie. But I also know how excited you are about having some children your age to play with, and thought you might just happen to forget."

Emma reached behind her and pulled open the door. The sound of happy voices in the entrance foyer reached them. It sounded so much like old times, Jessie thought, when her own mother and father were still alive, and relatives arrived for a holiday dinner. Of happier times, when everything seemed so safe and simple.

"Can I go now, Mama?"

Her daughter's voice tugged Jessie from her bittersweet thoughts. "Yes, go on," she said, meeting Emma's eager, questioning gaze. "But no playing outside until your hair's completely dry, okay?"

A head of light brown hair bobbed impatiently. "Yes, Mama."

She watched the six-year-old hurry off, hair-brush clenched in her little hand, and wondered if she could be counted on to spend even five minutes before the fire. Well, no matter, Jessie told herself. As long as she stayed inside, her hair would dry soon enough.

Turning her attention to the kitchen, she removed the sign on the door that said "Bath in Progress" and placed it back in the nearby cabinet. The old tin bathtub was quickly emptied and stored once again on the back porch off the kitchen. Used towels, soap, shampoo, and dirty clothes were stuffed into a big basket, and the floor hastily mopped dry. Then, after one final glance around the room to make certain all was in order, Jessie grabbed up the basket and headed down the hall to the stairs.

The house was already decorated with sprays of golden cottonwood and orange and brown scrub oak branches, the long dining room table, now positively huge with the addition of two extra leaves, graced with a centerpiece of yellow, orange, and green gourds, additional leaves, and two tall candles in ornately carved, walnut-stained wooden candlestick holders. Pumpkin pies were baking in the old cookstove, the odors of ginger, nutmeg, and cinnamon filling the air with a sweet, heady scent. The big tom turkey, already gutted and plucked, hung in the root cellar, ready to be put in the oven first thing in the morning. Spice cookies, filled with raisins and chopped pecans, waited on the kitchen table, and a big pot of mulled cider simmered on the cooktop, mugs and a ladle at the ready nearby. Beside the cider, another big pot of beef stew slowly cooked, this night's intended meal.

All was in readiness, Jessie thought as she climbed the stairs. Well, leastwise for this day. Tomorrow would bring its own challenges in the preparation of the majority of the Thanksgiving meal. But there'd also be additional women to help with that. Claire and Evan's two children—Sarah and Jacob—had just arrived with their respective spouses and children, two of which were close to Emma's age. Beth and her husband, Noah, were planning on coming in from Grand View by midmorning.

First thing, she'd have Conor and Sean carry

down Abby's convalescent chair and place it in the kitchen. Then, after she'd bathed and dressed Abby, she'd have them bring her down. It was where Abby deserved and needed to be, in the heart of her house, surrounded by the women she knew and loved, smack dab in the midst of all the crazy, joyous food preparations and special female camaraderie.

She smiled as she entered her bedroom and proceeded to hang up the towels to air dry on a line she had tied from one corner to the other on the far side of the room. So much went into the successful rehabilitation of any infirmity, and a very large part of it wasn't physical. A very large part of it was keeping one's patients' spirits up and showing them all the ways they could still be of use, even as one slowly but surely exercised their bodies to regain the necessary strength to do so. And, already, she knew the kind of woman Abby MacKay was, what kept her spirits up. Family—and her God—were everything to her.

Once, those had also been Jessie's priorities. She'd had such hopes and dreams when she had first wed Paul. She had felt so blessed, so grateful to the Lord for giving her such a wonderful husband. And he had been a wonderful husband to her for a time, showering her with everything she ever wanted, and more. She had soon become pregnant with Emma, however, and as each month passed thereafter, Paul had grown increasingly distant, until he was spending most nights away from home, returning in the morning with the reek of whiskey heavy about him.

Only after one horrible fight well into her pregnancy had he finally admitted he had never wanted children, and deeply resented the child who was to come. For a time, Jessie was devastated. Eventually, though, she convinced herself Paul was just frightened of the responsibilities of fatherhood, and all that would change once he held his firstborn in his arms.

Emma was a beautiful baby, perfectly formed, with the thickest thatch of dark blonde hair and the brightest, bluest eyes. It didn't make any difference to her father, though. When first presented with his new daughter, he had held her, briefly if impassively examined her, then handed her back to Jessie. He had never willingly touched her again.

By the time he killed himself on that fateful "Black Tuesday" over two years later, Jessie had all but given up hope of ever having her attentive, loving husband back again. His problem accepting his daughter, she had come to realize, went far deeper than just not wanting children. And all her prayers had gone unanswered, until she was on the brink of despair. Emma—and her own mother—were all that kept her from trying to follow where Paul had gone.

But, though Paul had been faithless and so apparently had God, Jessie couldn't bring herself to turn her back on her responsibilities, especially when one of them was her beloved daughter. Her daughter…Emma…who was such a gift, and just by being who she was, by being born, had ultimately saved her mother's life.

A gift…God's gift…to her, Jessie mused as she shut her bedroom door and headed back down the hall to the stairs. Despite Louise's hysterical accusations to the contrary when she'd learned of her only child's suicide, it had never been Jessie's fault that Paul was the man he was. No one, in the end, could've saved him if he didn't wish to be saved. Not family, not even God. That indeed was but another hope that had finally died an ignominious death. That Paul would someday find the Lord.

When she had first met Conor MacKay, he had told her that her name meant "the Lord's gift" and that she was truly the Lord's gift to them. Thinking back on it now, Jessie decided he had gotten things a bit twisted around. Far, far more than she was ever a gift to them, they had become a gift to her.

The Lord's gift.

Chapter Seven

An hour or so later, the children finally tired of playing in the house and asked permission to go outside. A stiff wind had picked up, and Jessie doubted they'd stay out long before getting too cold. Nevertheless, she also realized they needed to run off some of their excess energy. Bundled up so thoroughly they looked like plump little pumpkins, the youngsters soon headed from the house.

Jessie busied herself in the kitchen making bread to go with the supper stew and, an hour later, pulled two fat, perfectly browned loaves from the oven.

"Ye've certainly gotten the hang of Old Bess in record time," Claire observed from her spot at the table, where she and her daughter Sarah were sharing a pot of tea with Jessie and Abby. "When first I came to Culdee Creek, that stove was my bane and despair. I almost imagined it hated me, so difficult it made every meal I attempted to cook on or in it."

"I just treat it like a lot of stubborn, egotistical doctors I've worked with," Jessie said as she placed the bread on wire racks to cool. "Anticipate its every need and, in the doing, coax it into thinking it's doing what it wants, when really it's doing exactly what *I* want it to."

Sarah laughed, tossing back her head of auburn waves only a shade or two lighter than her mother's. "Don't let Aunt Beth hear you talking like that. She might take offense."

"Oh, I'd never speak that way of Dr. Starr." Jessie grinned at the woman who was only eight years her senior, and so closest in age of all the MacKay women present. "The little I've seen of her, I already know she's a lot different than most physicians. Plus, she came very highly recommended—"

Caleb and Annie, still dressed in their jackets, mittens, and hats, ran into the kitchen just then. "Boy, are we hungry!" Sarah's oldest son said. "That bread sure smells good. Can we have a slice with some butter?"

"No, you most certainly cannot," their mother was quick to reply. "Supper will be ready in another ten minutes, and you can wait. I was just about to come and call you all in anyway."

Jessie glanced through the open kitchen door down the hallway. "Where's Emma? She did come in with you, didn't she?"

Nine-year-old Caleb wrenched his ravenous gaze from the bread. "Huh? Oh no, she's still outside. She said she wanted to go down and say hello to the horses. She said Bucky's her special friend."

Bucky was the old pony Sean had been teaching her to ride. Still, Jessie thought as she removed her apron and laid it aside, she wasn't comfortable with her daughter down among the horses without an adult along. Especially since they were likely still out in their corrals, and Bucky shared one with the skittish and frequently mean-spirited stallion named Thunderbolt. Indeed, docile little Bucky was one of the few horses that could be paddocked with the big chestnut.

"Well, Emma's not allowed to be taking off to see the horses on her own," Jessie said, "so, if you'll excuse me, I need to go and fetch my daughter."

"Do you want me to tag along?" Sarah asked.

"Sure. If you think your mother can manage the children without us."

Claire chuckled. "Rather, ye mean guard the bread from them, don't ye?"

Jessie grinned. "Something like that."

"Get along with ye two," the older woman said, waving in the direction of the kitchen door. "Just don't tarry. I don't know how long I can hold off these two little vultures." She shot her grandchildren a conspiratorial look. "Or how long I'd even want to, for that matter. I mean, have ye ever seen two such bonny bairns in all yer life?"

Sarah took Jessie by the arm. "She won't last long. We'd better hurry."

They headed down the hall toward the entry foyer, where their coats hung on wooden pegs on the wall nearest the front door. As soon as they began putting on their coats, Sean, who was sitting in the parlor, saw them. He excused himself from the conversation he, his father, Evan, Evan's son Jacob, and Sarah's husband Seth were having.

"A bit chilly to be going out for a walk, isn't it?" he asked, drawing up before the two women.

"Most likely," Jessie replied as she finished buttoning her wool coat and tying a long, knit scarf about her head. "But Emma apparently decided to take it upon herself to go down and visit Bucky. And I'm not comfortable with her doing that without an adult around."

Concern darkened Sean's eyes, and he grabbed his canvas jacket off the rack. "Neither am I. I doubt the hands have begun putting the horses in the barn yet, which means—"

"That Bucky is still out with Thunderbolt," she finished for him.

He reached around her and pulled the front door open. An icy current of air whistled in. "Exactly. You don't mind if I get a head start, do you?" he asked, stepping around and in front of them even as he spoke. "Just in case, I'd like to get down to the corrals as quick as I can."

Sean was as worried as she was, Jessie realized. She nodded as she followed him onto the front porch. "Probably a good idea. It never hurts to—"

From down the road leading up to the house, a faint cry came from the direction of the corrals near the closest of the two barns. Sean shot her a sharp look, then took off running. Jessie scrambled down the steps after him, Sarah not far behind.

Her heart pounding in her breast, Jessie raced down the hill, but still Sean's lead grew larger and larger. Halfway there, she saw him reach the corrals, skirt them until he found the one that usually housed the pony and stallion, and begin to scramble up the wooden boards. As she drew near, she caught sight of her daughter crouched in the nearest corner of the corral, Thunderbolt, ears flattened, teeth bared, looming over her.

A scream clawed its way up her throat, but she clamped down on it before it could escape. Any unexpected noises just now might send the horse over the edge and into some killing frenzy. Instead, Jessie, uttering a series of frantic silent prayers, forced herself to walk to the other end of the corral from where Sean was now perched on the top of the fence above Emma, and climb up.

If she had to, she intended to clamber over and into the pen, distracting the horse any way she could away from her daughter. But only if

Sean couldn't handle things. He knew a lot better than she what the best tactic was in such situations.

His voice a low, soothing murmur, he spoke to the big stud horse as he slowly removed his jacket and laid it on the top rail. "I'm going to climb down now, Emma," he then said. "Once I get in front of you, you scoot between the boards. Okay, little miss?"

"Y-yes, sir," came the choked reply.

As he carefully swung his right leg over, Thunderbolt snorted and lunged for him. Jessie gasped. At the same instant, Sean grabbed his jacket and flung it over the horse's head.

"Now, Emma!" he shouted. "Move! Get through the fence!"

To her credit, the little girl didn't freeze up but immediately turned and scrambled through the two lowest boards. Jessie climbed down and ran to her daughter, pulling her into her arms.

With an enraged squeal and hoofs flailing the air, the stallion reared back. Shaking his head in an attempt to fling off the jacket , he fought for several seconds before finally freeing himself. Sean, however, didn't waste time watching to see if the animal was successful. He threw his leg back over the corral fence and jumped down.

"Don't you ever go near that horse again, do you hear me?" Jessie sobbed, a crazy mix of relief, love, and anger flooding her. "You scared the life out of me, you did!"

Emma was weeping even harder than her mother and didn't say anything, just clung to her for all she was worth. Neither of them heard Sean walk up to them, or realized he was near until he finally spoke.

"Are you all right, Emma?" he asked. "That old horse didn't hurt you, did he?"

"N-no, he didn't h-hurt me," she replied between hiccupping breaths, daring a glance up at him from the haven of her mother's arms. "Y-you saved m-me."

He *had* saved Emma, Jessie realized, gazing over her shoulder at him then. "Thank you. That was very, very brave."

Once the words left her lips, they suddenly seemed so meager an expression of gratitude. If something had happened to Emma…

He smiled lopsidedly at her. "I was really only

protecting my horse. If you'd seen the look on your face as you climbed up on that fence, you'd understand why I was in greater fear for Thunderbolt than for Emma."

His comment was meant as a joke, she instinctively knew, because he wasn't comfortable accepting gratitude, much less compliments. She smiled back at him through her tears and, in that moment, something passed between them. Something deep and joyous and good.

Before Jessie even had a chance to think, much less consider her impulsive act, she released her daughter, walked the few feet over to Sean, and, standing on tiptoe, kissed him on the cheek. "No, thank *you*. Thank *you*."

Surprise flashed in his eyes, then a wary pleasure. He touched the spot where her lips had been but a second ago.

"That was nice. Very nice."

Heat stole into Jessie's face. She looked away, and her glance slammed into Sarah's. In all the excitement, she must not have seen the other woman, who now stood several feet to the side, watching them both with careful consideration. Jessie felt the heat rush to her cheeks. She had forgotten that Sarah had followed them to the corrals.

"Come along, sweetheart," she said, making a big show of ignoring Sean by taking her daughter by the arm. "It's past time we got you back to the house."

"Yes, Mama," the little girl meekly replied.

As they strode past Sarah, however, Jessie shot her a warning look. "Not a word, do you hear me?" she bit out past clenched teeth. "Not a word about that kiss to anyone!"

The auburn-haired woman grinned, then fell into step beside her. "Not a word about how you kissed my uncle and he liked it? My lips are sealed." She chuckled. "Well, at least until I get back to the house, at any rate."

Around ten that evening and after everyone had finally turned in for the night, Jessie finished her daily entry in her journal. With a sigh, she laid down her pen and closed the book. By the orange glow of the single oil lamp on the table, she glanced around the tidy kitchen. Though the wind howled outside, the room was cozy and warm from Old Bess's fire.

Everything was in order for tomorrow's breakfast. Plates, glasses, and silverware were stacked on the sideboard, fresh grounds and water already filled the coffeepot, and extra firewood was stacked in the nearby box to help restart the stove in the morning. All that was left to do was bank the coals in the stove's firebox, and she could head off to bed.

She climbed to her feet. As she did, a faint cry came to her. Immediately, Jessie knew it was Emma, and knew she must be having a nightmare. Without hesitation, she hurried from the kitchen.

After the past few weeks, she had begun to hope her daughter's life had started to settle down enough that nightmares were becoming a thing of the past. What with the lack of worry over food and shelter since they had come to Culdee Creek, combined with the love and generous care the MacKays had showered on Emma, there indeed hadn't been any nightmares in a while. But she was likely being overly optimistic, Jessie thought as she took the stairs to the second floor two steps at a time.

The scare with the horses today notwithstanding, they had both been through some extended bad times. The wounds created by such pain and stress didn't heal overnight.

Even before she reached their bedroom door, Jessie heard Emma's muffled sobs. Hurrying inside, she headed straight for her daughter's bed.

"Oh, sweetheart, what happened?" she murmured as she sat down beside her. "Did you have a bad dream?"

"Uh-huh," the child said, flinging herself into her mother's arms. "I dreamed…I dreamed it was cold and dark and the wind was screaming. And…and then I saw that big, awful horse again, and this time I couldn't get away. And nobody came to save me. No one…not even y-you."

Jessie pulled Emma tightly to her. "I'll always be there to save you, sweetie. We're special pals, after all. No matter what, we'll always stick together."

Tear-bright eyes gazed up at her. "P-promise, Mama?"

She nodded. "Promise."

That finally seemed to satisfy the little girl. They sat there for a while, until Jessie could tell Emma was beginning to drowse again. Ever so gently, she laid her daughter in her bed and tucked the covers back around her. Then, pulling the rocking chair close, Jessie sat and watched until Emma fell asleep.

After a time, she began to feel drowsy herself. Her lids lowered. *I'll just stay here a little longer*, she thought. *Just in case Emma wakes…*

The next thing she knew, Jessie jerked awake. Momentarily disoriented, she looked around. Save for some sporadically cloud-shrouded moonlight, the room was dark. What was she doing in the rocker? What time was it?

Recollection of Emma's nightmare returned. She looked to her daughter, who was still sleeping soundly. Jessie shoved from the rocker and walked to her nightstand. The small alarm clock's hands stood at 11:10. She had dozed off for nearly an hour.

Jessie turned back her bedcovers, then walked to the cupboard to retrieve her nightgown. As she did, she realized that not only had she not banked the cookstove, but also she had left her journal on the kitchen table.

Though the odds were strong she'd be one of the first to return to the kitchen in the morning, Jessie didn't want to risk someone taking a peek at her journal. Not that she feared Conor or even Sean doing so, but there were other guests in the house now. They might not realize what they were reading until they had delved further than she would've wanted anyone to know of her private thoughts.

With a sigh, Jessie turned and headed for the door. One more trip downstairs was necessary before she could finally get to bed on what had been an emotionally tumultuous day. She was surprised, however, when she drew close to the kitchen, to find the door to it closed. She didn't recall shutting it behind her...

The reason for the closed door was immediately evident the moment Jessie pushed it open and walked in. There, in the glow of the oil lamp, a man, his back turned, stood at the sink, emptying a bucket of water from the tin bathtub. Clothed only in his denims, Sean stood there, the broad expanse of his back gleaming with a light sheen of moisture. A very broad, bare, and most attractively muscled back.

Her throat went dry. Apparently Sean had just finished up his bath. She inched away, hoping to make an escape before he realized he was no longer alone. Unfortunately, the door had swung shut behind her. Jessie slammed into it with a thud.

Sean whirled around. In the dim light, it must have taken him a moment to recognize his unexpected visitor. Once he did, though, he grinned.

"If you came to offer your assistance," he drawled lazily, "you're too late. But I suppose there's always the possibility of a rain check…"

Chapter Eight

Her mouth agape, Jessie stared at him for several speechless seconds. If he had been unexpectedly disturbing with his back turned, he was downright devastating facing her. All lean, rippling muscle, from his broad chest and strong arms to his well-defined abdomen, Sean MacKay was undeniably a man in his prime. As she gazed at him, something Jessie had thought long dead flared to life. Something akin to yearning and, most unexpectedly, desire.

"A—a rain check?" she finally managed to sputter, wrenching her thoughts back to a far more safe and sane reality. "You're joking, aren't you?"

He shrugged. "I guess I'd better be. If not, you'll probably take me for some arrogant cur, if not an outright lecher. And then where would our fledgling friendship be?"

She eyed him uncertainly. Though Sean probably had every right to be a bit arrogant, considering—clothed or partially unclothed—he could make any woman's heart skip a beat, it wouldn't do to apprise him of that. Wouldn't do at all.

"It'd be down the drain for sure," Jessie replied, then forced a strained laugh. "I'm sorry for barging in on you. I just didn't expect anyone else to be up this late. And, besides, you didn't put the sign on the door."

"Probably for the same reason you barged in on me. I also didn't expect anyone up this late. And there sure wasn't going to be any time tomorrow to get a bath. Everyone's usually up at the crack of dawn on Thanksgiving Day. And, once the womenfolk take over the kitchen…"

She nodded, finally beginning to feel on more stable ground. "We do have a tendency to monopolize the kitchen, don't we? Of course, it's only to get those special foods cooked that all you menfolk seem to crave."

"Yeah, reckon we are a demanding lot." Sean walked to the table and picked up the shirt hanging on one of the chair backs. "Be assured, though, that all your efforts are very much appreciated, especially once we sit down to the Thanksgiving feast."

She watched him don his shirt and, for an instant, Jessie's attention was once more distracted. Muscles clenched then expanded as he shoved first one arm, then the other into the shirtsleeves. As he began to button the front closed, her glance next went to his long fingers, the nails trimmed short and neat. To his hands that were as surprisingly refined as they appeared strong.

"Er, is there something wrong?" Sean finally asked. "Did I button my shirt all cockeyed?"

Jessie blushed and quickly shook her head. "No, the shirt's fine. I was just…just thinking about something else." Unable to meet his now searching gaze, she glanced around and found her journal lying on the table. "I…I just came down to get this." She strode to the table and grabbed up the book.

His mouth quirked, and she couldn't tell if it was in wryness or pain. "Charlotte used to keep a journal too," he said softly. "In all the years of our marriage, she never let me read a word of it."

"Well, it is a private thing." An awkward silence settled between them then. Finally, clutching the journal to her, Jessie glanced toward the door. "I suppose it's time I was going. I'm sorry to have disturbed you."

"You didn't disturb me, Jessie. Far from it."

Even as she turned to leave, the husky timbre of his voice drew her up short. She looked back at him.

"Well…I'm glad." Suddenly, Jessie didn't know what else to say, so she uttered the very next thing that entered her mind. "Thank you again for what you did for Emma today. I…I don't know what I would've done if something had happened to her."

"You're welcome. We all look out for each other here at Culdee Creek. And I've got a lot of making up to do, for how I treated you when you first came here."

She gave a small, dismissive wave of her hand. "It's forgotten. What matters now is that we move forward, and make the most of that."

He walked over to stand before her. "I agree."

Before she could react, much less even

fathom what he was about to do, Sean reached up, slid his hand behind her head and, leaning down, kissed her. His mouth was gentle; his lips moved tenderly over hers. For a sharp, sweet instant, Jessie thought she might faint from the sheer pleasure of it.

Her knees buckled. If not for Sean's quick response in pulling back and grabbing her by both arms, she likely would've fallen. His swift reaction, combined with the firm hold he had on her, jerked her back to reality.

"Wh-what was that all about?" she managed to stammer.

"That was just me moving forward. And, since you took the initiative earlier today, I thought now it was my turn."

"Uh, well, my kiss was one of gratitude, given on impulse, for what you'd done for Emma," Jessie said, shrugging out of his now loose clasp and stepping back from him. "What exactly was the reason for yours?"

"Does a man need a reason to kiss a beautiful woman?" Amusement twinkled now in his dark, luminous eyes.

She studied him warily. What was going on

here? The change in Sean, at least in regards to her, seemed to be evolving at an ever-increasing pace. Problem was, though a part of her was intrigued, even excited by his response, another part of her warned that it was too soon and even bordered on the improper, considering he was the son of her patient. Had she set something unseemly into motion today with her innocent kiss?

"I'm very flattered that you think me beautiful," she carefully began, "but this is all happening so fast. I mean, it wasn't that long ago that we were barely talking. And I hope you won't take offense, but though a friendly relationship with my employer and family is appropriate, anything else isn't."

"It was only a kiss, Jessie," Sean said, smiling. "Still, I respect that you feel the need to maintain a professional distance. I just hope you won't take offense with my saying you shouldn't look at a man like you have tonight at me, if you only want a friendly relationship."

At his honest if blunt statement, a wild muddle of emotions whirled within her. Though she was relieved that he evidently wasn't angry at what she had said, she was also a bit miffed at his brazen assessment of the effect he'd had on her earlier, standing there bare-chested and so heart-stoppingly attractive. An assessment that, to make matters even worse, was shamefully accurate.

"You're right, of course. My behavior was un-professional. It won't happen again. Neither the looks or any more kissing." She hesitated, won-dering if she should explain further or not. "I'm not usually…this way. You just surprised me and…and I'm still unsettled over today's incident with Emma. Please forgive me."

"It's forgiven." He stared down at her with a warm, tender expression. "I'll confess I was kind of surprised myself, kissing you, I mean. I haven't kissed another woman in a very, very long while, not to mention had one look at me like you did. I guess I also lost my head for a minute."

His words confused her. He hadn't kissed a woman or had one look at him with desire in a very long while? But what of his wife? What of other women in Grand View, or wherever else he might've traveled?

She almost asked him those very questions,

then caught herself. She'd no right to know such things. Indeed, it wasn't wise for her to know. Already, she risked getting too emotionally involved. Already, things were beginning to move far too fast.

"No harm was done, I suppose," Jessie said. "We're both adults and understand how insidious loneliness can be, especially after both once having spouses. But we both must also remember what really matters. That I'm here only because I didn't have anywhere else to go, and you and your family needed help with your mother."

"Not to mention you're afraid I'm the sort who enjoys seducing the hired help."

Embarrassment flooded her. "No, it's not that at all. I don't think you're that sort of man. I just meant—"

"Oh, come on, Jessie," Sean said, his patience apparently at an end. "You hardly yet know what sort of man I am."

"I know what sort of people your parents are, and I can only assume you're cut of the same cloth."

"Well, that'll get you in a lot of trouble. Assuming, I mean." He stepped back, his gaze grim, his mouth hard. "You know nothing of where I've been, what I've done. And you only think you understand about my marriage to Charlotte. But you don't understand anything. Not anything at all."

Stung by the sudden bitterness, Jessie clutched her journal to her chest. "You're right," she said at last. "There's still a lot I don't know about you, Sean, or what experiences formed you as a man. But I do know you're honest and that you'd risk your life for the sake of a little girl. I also know you're loyal and love your family. And I can guess you've been hurt deeply, maybe even betrayed by someone you were close to, and that you don't give your trust lightly."

She paused, cut short by the unnatural sheen to his eyes. Were those tears? If so, she was striking too close to home. Too close to a place neither of them apparently wished to go, yet, conversely, a place neither could seem to avoid.

"I'm sorry." Jessie sighed and looked toward the ceiling before once more meeting his gaze. "I don't mean to push or pry. But I think I know a decent man when I meet him. And I told you before, I make up my own mind about people."

"So nothing I can say will warn you off?" The vestiges of a smile played now about his lips.

"I trust you, Sean. Enough said."

He didn't reply for a long while, only looked at her until Jessie almost imagined he was trying to probe the depths of her soul. Somehow, though, it didn't unsettle or frighten her. Somehow, instead, it felt oddly comforting, even reassuring.

"Well," he finally said, "I thank you for that. And from here on out, I'll try to be worthy of that trust. Can't speak for the past, but from here on out…"

"Fair enough." She grinned, all at once strangely happy and relieved. "Now, it's time I really was getting back upstairs to Emma."

She turned to leave when, once more, Sean halted her.

"Jessie?"

"Yes, Sean?" She glanced back over her shoulder.

"You know it's going to be hard to keep from kissing you again."

In spite of her best efforts to quash it, joy flamed brightly within her. "But you will try, won't you?"

He dragged in a deep, shuddering breath. "Yes, I'll do that much. I'll try."

"Here." As Sean pulled up in front of Gates Mercantile, Jessie dug into her handbag for the scraps of cotton feed-sack fabric Claire had given her. "These are the prints she wants you to match if you can." Leaning over Emma, she handed them to him. "She said she needed at least ten bags of chicken feed's worth of at least two of the prints, if you can get them."

Sean put the farm truck in park and took the proffered bits of cloth. "I could be a while at this, you know. Last time Claire sent me looking for specific patterns, I must have spent an hour and moved over fifty sacks of chicken feed to find the exact ones she was looking for."

"Well, she said she desperately needed those particular patterns to finish a quilt she's making for a Christmas gift. And, considering Christmas is only a week away…"

He sighed and rolled his eyes. "I'll do my best. That's all any man can do."

"I know you will." Jessie smiled. "Don't rush. I've got a long list of items to get for all the

Christmas baking Claire and I are going to start on tomorrow."

"And I want to look at the toys," Emma piped up just then. "So I can write Santa and tell him what I want for Christmas."

Jessie bit her lip and exchanged a pained look with Sean. "Sweetheart, I don't know how much Santa will be able to bring this Christmas—"

"Jessie." Sean reached over and, palm down, offered her something.

She took the wad, covered with a piece of paper, and closed her hand around it. "What's this?"

He put a finger to his lips. "Look at it later. And use it for her." He nodded toward Emma.

"Sean, I can't," Jessie replied, an inkling of what lay inside the paper filling her. "I'm only working for room and board, and have no way to—"

"We'll sort it all out later," he said. "Who knows? Maybe you can break a few horses for me, or help out in the barn. There are always stalls to muck out, horses to groom, and tack to clean, you know."

"Sure," she said with a laugh, shoving the money in her coat pocket. "I think I have some spare time after ten o'clock every night to maybe six in the morning. How would that suit you?"

He grinned. "As I said. We'll sort it out." He made a shooing motion with his hand. "Now, get on with you two. If all goes well, I'll be back in an hour with those feed sacks Claire's wanting."

Jessie reached for the door handle. "We'll be waiting outside for you."

"No, wait inside," Sean said as a freshened wind brought the beginnings of the snowstorm that had been forming over the distant mountains all day. "From the looks of those clouds, the snow will start to pile up fast. And I don't want to come back to find two snow ladies frozen outside the mercantile."

Emma giggled. "There's no such thing as snow ladies. It's snowmen. You're so funny, Mr. MacKay. You make me laugh."

He tipped his Stetson. "My pleasure, ma'am."

"I like him, Mama," Emma said as Jessie opened the door, climbed out, then turned to her daughter. "He's my very best of friends."

Over her daughter's shoulder as she helped her from the truck, Jessie met Sean's smiling gaze. Though he had been true to his word and managed not to kiss her in the ensuing weeks since their Thanksgiving eve encounter in the kitchen, and she had tried her best to maintain a professional if friendly distance, they had nevertheless grown closer and closer. So close of late, that every time he came near, Jessie's heart began a crazed pounding in her breast and she found her palms sweating and breathing going ragged.

It was crazy, how wildly her feelings about him swung. One minute she found herself pulling back, warning caution over and over even as she felt herself inexorably drawn to him, and the next, her heart soared with happiness just to be with him. And he was no help whatsoever in steadying her unruly emotions. Just one glimpse of Sean, all tall, virile, handsome man, or one boyishly crooked grin sent her way, and she forgot everything. Everything but him.

"He's my very good friend too," Jessie replied, wrenching her gaze from the dark-haired man in the truck and back to her daughter. She paused to shut the truck door and wave at Sean as he drove off, then smiled down at Emma. "Still, we don't know how much longer we'll be living at Culdee Creek. And once we leave, we might not see Mr. MacKay much anymore. You do realize this, don't you, sweetheart?"

"But why do we ever have to leave?" Big blue eyes widened in bewilderment. "Why can't you just marry Mr. MacKay? Why can't he be my father? Then we can live at the ranch forever."

Jessie stared down at her daughter. She had been so caught up in her own tumultuous feelings about Sean MacKay, she hadn't given much thought to what Emma must have been thinking about their growing relationship. Emma, who, for all practical purposes, had never known a father's attention and love. Who must be starving for everything Sean had been showering upon her these past weeks.

"Well, for one thing, neither Mr. MacKay nor I are looking to get married right now." Jessie squatted and took her daughter by both arms. "And, for another, I've got other plans for us, and they don't include either a husband for me or a father for you just yet. Let's get our lives settled down a bit first, then maybe I'll start looking for a father for you, okay?"

As if she were trying to sort things through in her mind, Emma frowned. "But Jesus has already done all the hard work for us, Mama," she finally pronounced, a triumphant smile spreading across her face. "He brought us here and found a very nice man for you and me, besides all the other very nice people who live on the ranch. What else do we need?"

"It's not quite as simple as all that, sweetheart." She sighed and shook her head. "You'll understand that better someday, but for now you just need to trust me in this."

"And I think *you* need to trust Jesus more, Mama!" Her daughter gave a disgusted snort. "Maybe if you trust Jesus more, things won't get so messed up."

"Well, you just might be right about that." Jessie stood, took her hand, and tugged her toward the front door. "I'll think about it some, okay? In the meanwhile, we've got a lot of shopping to do before Mr. MacKay returns, so we'd better get to work."

Seemingly mollified by her mother's promise to think about things, Emma nodded solemnly. "Yes, we sure do have a lot of work to do. Let's go, Mama!"

Once inside the mercantile, Emma lost no time

heading for the colorful display of children's toys, leaving Jessie to see to the shopping list. Though Culdee Creek Ranch supplied all needed meats, from beef and pork to chicken and their eggs, along with milk, cream, and butter from the small herd of dairy cows, plus sufficient root crops that stored well for many months in the root cellar and myriad canned vegetables from a large summer garden, not to mention bartering local farmers for wheat flour, there were still items that had to be purchased. The list in Jessie's hand was long: salt, sugar, and various spices; baking powder for the Christmas cookies; toothpaste and three new toothbrushes; a bottle of aspirin; shaving cream and razor blades for the men; milk of magnesia and talcum powder to help in Abby's care; a box of nickel-plated safety pins; and a card of steel hairpins for Claire. And then, with the money Sean had given her for Emma—two dollars, she noted as she finally dug into her pocket and pulled out the bills—there was now an opportunity for some store-bought gifts to accompany the stuffed Scotty dog and pretty blue print dress she had made under Claire's tutelage from the older woman's large stash of feed-sack prints.

After delivering her list to the general store's clerk, who immediately set to filling it, Jessie made a beeline for the small shoe display. There she found a pair of sensible, laced, black leather oxfords for eighty-eight cents. For the past year, Emma had worn shoes she had not only all but outgrown, but that possessed soles consisting of several layers of cardboard. Thanks to Sean's generosity, at least now her daughter would start the new year with a decent pair of new shoes on her feet. And, best of all, there would still be over a dollar left for an actual toy or two.

As surreptitiously as she could, she moved closer to observe which toys Emma seemed to take the most interest in. Her daughter lingered over a selection of books, then some boxes of puzzles, and as soon as she finally headed to a rack of girl's dresses located off in a corner, Jessie quickly scooted over to them.

A colorful scene of children skating on an icy pond caught Jessie's eye. It was a box of one hundred wooden pieces, just complicated enough to keep a six-year-old busy for at least a few days. She grabbed it up, along with two storybooks that she could first read to her daughter but were also easy enough that Emma would soon be able to read herself, then hurried to the store counter. After paying for all the purchases, she had them wrapped before Emma could notice.

The clerk hadn't quite finished with the list of items for the ranch, the cost of which would be applied to Culdee Creek's running account. Paper bag full of Emma's precious Christmas gifts in her hand, Jessie next ambled over to examine the women's dresses. As she longingly fingered a pretty, bright green, two-piece woolen sweater set with matching long, fitted knit skirt, she noted the wool felt beret sitting on a shelf above the clothes rack.

What a cute outfit that would make, she thought, just as the front door bell tinkled, signaling that another customer had walked in. She glanced over her shoulder and saw it was Mr. Rowles from the train depot, accompanied by an older woman. She waved and turned back to examine the price tag of the knit set. It cost two dollars and ninety-eight cents. Two dollars and ninety-eight cents more than she had, or expected to have anytime soon.

With a sigh, Jessie walked away from an outfit

that, when Paul was still alive, she could've bought three or four versions of without an instant's hesitation. Instead, she made a beeline to the bolts of fabric stacked on tall shelves against a far wall.

"Don't see much of you about town these days," a deep voice she recognized as that of Howard Rowles came from behind her a few minutes later.

Jessie turned around and smiled at the heavyset man before her glance settled on the woman standing beside him. "My name's Jessica Ashmore," she said, offering her hand to the woman. "But I haven't had the pleasure yet of meeting you, I'm afraid."

The plump, gray-haired woman with sad eyes shot Howard a wry glance. "And likely you never will, if I depend on my husband to make the introductions." She took Jessie's hand. "I'm Mary Rowles."

Howard flushed. "I'm sorry. My manners are rather lacking these days. Mary, this is the new nurse who's taking care of Abby MacKay. The one I told you about who came from Baltimore with her little girl."

"I gathered that," his wife dryly replied. She shook Jessie's hand, then released it. "Pleased to finally make your acquaintance."

Jessie smiled. "Pleased to make yours too."

There was a long pause, then Howard cleared his throat. "No other job prospects in the offing, I gather?"

"No, none yet, but I'm hopeful that might change after the holidays," Jessie replied. "In the meanwhile, I'm very fortunate to have work at Culdee Creek."

He frowned. "Oh yes. They're good folk... well, most of them are, anyways. I've seen you in town with Sean MacKay a few times. Just a word of advice. He's not all he might appear."

She looked at him quizzically, even as she noted how Mary's eyes grew wide and then she seemed to withdraw into herself. "Sean seems pretty straightforward to me. Kind, considerate, and very gallant."

Howard made a disgusted sound. "Gallant, is he? I see he hasn't lost his appeal with the ladies. My advice, though, is to look a little deeper and past that pretty face of his. You'll find there's not much there, at least nothing that amounts to anything."

"And *you're* pretty full of unwanted advice these days, aren't you, Howard?"

At the unexpected sound of Sean's voice, both Jessie and Howard Rowles jerked around while Mary stood there as if she'd grown roots into the ground.

"Oh, you're back already," Jessie cried in delight. "That was…" At his furious expression, directed not at her but at the older man, her voice faded.

"Someone's got to warn this little lady about you," Howard snarled, glaring back at Sean. "And it's evidently not going to be one of your family, is it?"

"There's nothing to warn her about," Sean snapped. He took Jessie by the arm. "Are you finished with your shopping? If so, we need to head back before the roads become impassable."

Jessie glanced to the long counter where, even now, the clerk was putting down a box full of her requested items. "Sure. I just need to go and pick that up"—she gestured in the direction of the counter—"and then we can be on our—"

"I'll get it," Sean brusquely cut her off. "In the meanwhile, why don't you gather up Emma and meet me at the truck?"

"Okay." She glanced hesitantly from one man to the other.

Sean shot Howard Rowles one final, seething look, then turned on his heel and stalked away. Jessie watched him go, then forced a smile for the older couple.

"It was good to see you again, Mr. and Mrs. Rowles. You'll excuse me, though, if I must take my leave. We've got to get home…the storm and all."

"Good to see you again too, Mrs. Ashmore." Howard looked in Sean's direction. When he saw that the younger man's attention was momentarily diverted from them, he leaned close to Jessie. "I'm not usually one to stick my nose in other folks' business, ma'am, but since no one seems to have the guts to tell you the truth, I will. Sean MacKay's a coward and deserter. Just ask him sometime about what happened to him in the Great War. Ask him, then come to me and I'll tell you the rest of the story."

With that, he took his wife by the arm and headed across the store. Sean picked up the box of supplies just then and strode back to her.

"I thought you were going to fetch Emma," he said, an angry light still smoldering in his eyes.

She hadn't seen him so tightly strung in a long while. "I'm sorry. We'll meet you outside in just a minute." She hurried to her daughter. "Time to go, sweetheart."

"Aw, Mama," the little girl moaned. "Do we have to? I still want to look around some more."

"Yes, we do." Jessie reached down to button up her daughter's coat. "We need to get back to the ranch."

Emma sighed. "Oh, all right then."

The box of supplies, along with the bags of chicken feed, was already firmly tied down in the truck bed beneath a sturdy tarp, and Sean awaited her in the truck. They climbed in, and he wasted little time shifting the vehicle into gear and heading down Main Street. For the longest while, Jessie didn't know what to say to him. The hard set to his lips and tightly clenched jaw did little to convey any willingness on his part to talk, either.

Eventually, however, she couldn't bear the tension-fraught silence any longer. "I'm sorry if I caused you distress by talking with Howard Rowles," she finally blurted out, half turning in the seat to face him. "I didn't know there was bad blood between you."

His answering laugh was harsh. "Oh, there's a lot more than bad blood between us. Not only is he my late best friend's father, he's also my former father-in-law."

It took her a moment to digest that startling bit of information. "Your wife Charlotte's father?"

"One and the same," Sean gritted out. "And, to be sure, no longer any friend of mine."

Chapter Nine

Sean avoided Jessie the rest of the day. It was bad enough he'd had to run into Howard Rowles and his wife in town, which invariably always ended in an exchange of angry words. Well, angry words with Howard, anyway. Mary, as usual, could barely meet his gaze. He'd never quite figured that out, even after all these years. Likely she just couldn't bear to look at him, or face all the painful memories his presence stirred.

Now, though, after that unfortunate but inevitable encounter, Jessie surely had a good inkling about that dark time in his past. Well, maybe not all the details, but enough, he was sure, to cast doubts in her mind about him.

Howard, vindictive old coot that he was, hadn't bothered to lower his voice much when he'd said his final piece to Jessie. Even from as far away as the counter, Sean's acute hearing had heard it all. She knew now of that black cloud of cowardice and desertion that would likely hang over him the rest of his life.

His avoidance of her was nonetheless only a delaying action, one Sean knew he couldn't stretch out for too long. As a friend, he owed her some sort of explanation. As a woman for whom he had come to care deeply, she deserved the whole, unvarnished, painful truth. Their relationship had hit a wall. It couldn't progress further until she knew the full story. *If* there were any relationship left to them, once she knew.

She didn't press him, though, he thought, sending her covert glances that evening as they all gathered in the parlor around the battery-powered radio. First, they listened to the humorous Jack Benny, then Burns and Allen on *The Guy Lombardo Show*, before finishing with a program featuring the down-home wit and sharp political satire of Will Rogers, which elicited a lot of laughs and more than a few concurring nods.

Sean knew Jessie well enough by now to recognize that she was in a pensive mood. It wasn't much of a stretch to guess he was at least part of the reason.

Finally, the family evening came to an end. Jessie rose to put Emma to bed while Conor helped Abby walk to the stairs, where he'd then carry her up to their bedroom. Sean waited until his parents left the room, then hurried over to Jessie.

"When you're finished with Emma"—he laid a hand on her arm—"would you come back down here? I need…" He paused, suddenly not sure how to word his request. "There's more to the story than Rowles led you to believe today," he finally said. "I'd like you to hear both sides."

She met his imploring gaze with a troubled one of her own. "I'd like to hear both sides too. It'll take me about a half hour, though, to get Emma settled in. We say prayers, and then I read her a story."

Relief filled him. She was willing, even open, to hearing his side. "I can wait."

"In a half hour then," she said and walked away with her daughter.

By the time Jessie returned, Sean had mentally tossed around countless ways to explain what had happened to him in the war, and hadn't gotten much for his efforts but sweaty palms and a churning stomach. To make matters worse, the moment she stepped back into the parlor, any and all preplanned explanations fled him.

No woman had ever been able simultaneously to make his mind go blank and his heart soar like Jessie Ashmore did. Yet, once she was near, once she smiled that smile that made him feel like he was the only man in the world, Sean found he could talk to her about any and everything. Found that he felt safe and understood and so very, very special.

But not tonight. Tonight, he sensed her reserve. Tonight, he sensed if she found what he told her displeasing, or if she doubted his word, he might lose her forever. And, though he also knew there might be no way ultimately to prevent it, Sean nevertheless dreaded the potential parting.

"Would you like to sit over on the sofa?" he asked, indicating the big, plaid piece of furniture. "It'd be more comfortable than standing."

She shook her head. "I've been sitting all evening. If you don't mind, I'd like a bit of fresh air."

"Well…sure. It's going to be pretty cold outside, though. And with all the snow, we can't go far."

"The front porch will do me fine."

He helped her on with her coat, then shrugged into his. As soon as they stepped out onto the front porch, Sean realized he was as glad to be out there as she seemed to be. The storm had passed a few hours ago, taking with it the heavy clouds and winds. A full moon shone, illuminating the thick layer of freshly fallen snow. The air was crisp but not unpleasantly so, the night calm, silent.

As the minutes ticked by in wordless contemplation, everything seemed to take on a sharper focus, gain a far more acute perspective. He was what he was, Sean reminded himself. Things hadn't always turned out as he might have hoped, but he had always done what he thought was best, tried to be honorable and fair even if, he added with a wry smile, glancing briefly at Jessie, it sometimes took him time to come around to it. She would either understand and accept what he had to say, or not. All he could do was tell her the truth.

Shoving his hands into his jacket pockets, Sean expelled a deep breath and began. "I knew Carl Rowles all my life. His family's small farm is halfway between Culdee Creek and Grand View, so our parents took turns taking us both to school. We were the best of friends, did nearly everything together. And, once Charlotte, Carl's little sister, got old enough, she joined in. Well," he added with a sad smile, "as much as we'd let her anyway. When she grew into a young woman, then I was more than willing to let her join in as much as she wished.

"Carl and I were both pretty wild and headstrong in those days. When the U.S. finally entered into the war in April, 1917, we were among the first to enlist." Sean gave a sardonic laugh. "None of our parents were overly happy with our decision. My folks had been pushing since I finished high school for me to go to college. And, in retrospect, I think Carl's parents saw problems ahead if their son got too far from their influence."

"What kind of problems?" Jessie asked.

He shrugged. "Carl was kind of an unsteady sort. Except for me, he never stuck to anyone or thing for long. And when the going got hard, he tended to find some way to shirk or even avoid his responsibilities. He'd lost several jobs since he had dropped out of high school a year before we were both to graduate. He couldn't get along with his father well enough to help him much on the farm, either. Guess Carl just preferred to take the easy way out. For most of his life, he managed to do so. Well, at least until he joined the army anyway.

"We made it through training, and even all the way to France as part of the American Expeditionary Force, before Carl started balking at the hardship and restrictions. He began to get into trouble, minor things at first, but with each punishment, he pushed back all the harder. It got so he was spending more time restricted to the barracks when he wasn't in the field. Finally, a little over a year after we got to France, it all came to a head. One night Carl decided he'd had it and made plans to hightail it to Paris, where he intended to hide out until the war was over."

"You mean he deserted?"

Sean nodded. "Yeah. That was his plan. He had told me about it before, but I thought he was just dreaming. You know, wishful thinking. But when I got back to the barracks that night and found his note…well, I went after him. Times were bad then, and some other men had been deserting. Most had been caught and brought back, some court-martialed and others put in front of the firing squad. With Carl's sorry record, I was afraid what his punishment this time might be."

"So, you weren't deserting yourself, just going after your friend to bring him back before he was caught."

"Yeah, that's my story anyway." He made a disgusted sound. "Not the same one Howard Rowles believes, though."

"No, not from what he told me." Jessie turned to him. "So what happened? Did you get Carl back before his disappearance was discovered?"

He shook his head, the old, familiar sense of defeat and despair flooding him. "He wouldn't come back, no matter how hard I tried to convince him. We got into a fight, and he accidentally knocked me out. When I came to, the military police had caught up with us. Found out Carl had told them that *he* had gone after *me* to bring me back. It was also the story he apparently told his parents, during the time we were both in the stockade prior to our trial. Howard claims he still has that letter, anyway. And I don't have Carl's note. Fool that I was, before I went after him, I burned it in the hopes of protecting him."

"Still, it doesn't make a lot of sense," Jessie said, "though I guess it's a natural tendency of parents always to want to believe the best of their children."

"I guess he kept hoping Carl would finally grow up. Maybe thought he had." Sean sighed. "In the end, at least the army chose to believe my story over Carl's. It was a hollow victory, though. If I'd realized what Carl's punishment would be, I would've let his story ride. He was executed, and I court-martialed."

"You would've risked a lot, admitting to deserting. Maybe even died instead."

"Maybe. But I should've thought about it more. With his miserable record, this time Carl had dug himself a hole he couldn't get out of. And no one, not me or his father, could save him."

"He wasn't your responsibility, Sean." She laid a hand on his arm. "Sooner or later, a person's got to accept the consequences of his actions."

"Yeah, I know. But it still hurts. And even

though Carl's long dead and buried, the consequences of his actions are continuing to hurt a lot of people. Not just me, but his parents, and my parents too. And it destroyed my marriage to Charlotte."

Jessie was silent for a long moment. "She never forgave you, did she? For what she believed you'd done to her brother."

"Pretty much. We married just before I left for training. She was seventeen; I was nineteen, and we were so in love." Sean gave a soft, bitter laugh. "Neither set of parents was overly happy about that, either. Both wanted us to wait until the war was over. But we didn't. We eloped."

"And in all the years since then, she never forgave you, yet remained married to you?"

"Sounds strange, doesn't it?" He looked away, far out into the moonlit, snow-covered night. "I loved her in spite of it all, and kept hoping. And Charlotte…well, I don't know why she stayed. Maybe she still loved me in some sort of sad, tormented way, or maybe she just hoped she could find a way to cope with it all by bearing children upon which to shower her love. But even that didn't happen. She miscarried twice, and then had two stillborns. After that, well, she refused to have anything to do with me. We lived in the same house but, for all practical purposes, led separate lives until she died two years ago of influenza."

"I'm sorry," she said softly. "I…I don't know what else to say."

"There isn't anything *to* say. It's the hand I was dealt, and I have to make the best of it."

"But have you? Made the best of it, I mean?"

It wasn't the response he had expected from Jessie, and yet, somehow, it was more condemning than any he had conceived in his worst imaginings. "Exactly what do you mean by that?" he demanded in barely contained irritation. "What more can I do?"

"Forgive. Let the anger go. And finally find a peace, a completion, in that."

Sean's laugh was bitter. "Forgive? *I* was the one sinned against every step of the way, yet you expect *me* to forgive? Well, I'm not some dog who keeps crawling back to lick the foot of the person who kicked him! I might not have much left, but I still have my pride."

"Ah yes," she all but whispered. "Pride. It

serves us all so well, doesn't it, until we one day discover it didn't gain us anything of what we truly needed."

Her words left him totally bewildered. How and when had his tale of Carl's betrayal and Charlotte's choosing her family over him transformed into an issue of his pride and need to forgive? All he had wanted tonight was to explain his side of the story, gain her acceptance, and then resume where they had left off. Now, though, it seemed to have turned into some morality play in which he was supposed to forgive the lack of faithfulness in others and choose a godly life over one of evil. Yet, how had he done any evil? And, more to the point, when had even God been faithful in any of this?

"Well, now you've heard my side of the story," Sean said, the sense of being judged yet again burning through him like gall. "If it's still not enough to reassure you about me, then there's not much more I can say. Just don't load more misery on my shoulders by holding me to your exalted standards. I am what I am. Take it or leave it."

He turned to Jessie then, hoping, searching her face for any sign she believed him, that her doubts were finally assuaged. Maybe it was the shadows that hid her response, or maybe she purposely cloaked it, but he couldn't tell anything. Resignation filled him. She would either understand and accept what he had to tell her, or not. There was nothing more he could do.

For the first time, Sean noticed she was shivering. It *had* gotten cold. How long had they been standing out here anyway?

"Come on. You've heard more than your fair share for one night." He took her by the arm. "They say everything seems better in the morning."

She looked up at him, nodded. "So they say. And you're right. I've had more than enough to think on today." With that, Jessie accompanied him back into the house and, after bidding him good night, wordlessly made her way upstairs.

The next morning, Jessie got the phone on its second ring because she just happened to be in the kitchen. For some unknown reason, however, she didn't first register that the phone call was for her when the caller asked, "May I please speak with Jessica Ashmore?"

Afterward, she made herself a cup of tea and took a seat at the kitchen table. Through the window over the sink, Jessie watched as big, fat, lazy snowflakes drifted past to join their compatriots on the undulating mounds of foot-high drifts.

Strange, she mused, how timing was frequently everything when it came to making certain life decisions. Only yesterday evening, she had learned not only why Sean rarely went to town and chose to live a fairly isolated life on the ranch, but finally more of what were some very painful parts of his past. There were always two sides—or more—to every dispute, though. Did the truth lie more on one side or the other, or somewhere between, in that nebulous land of personal bias and perspective?

And now, to make matters even more complicated, she had just received a job offer to work as a floor nurse on the surgical ward at Bethel General Hospital, starting the second week of January. A full-time job in Colorado Springs, paying even more than she would've made working as Dr. Starr's office nurse. Yet, though this job seemed the answer to all her problems, she had still asked for a few days to consider the offer. A few days…to consider exactly what?

The memory of last night, of Sean's reaction to her suggestion that he needed to find some way to forgive those who had maligned him, lingered at the edge of her thoughts. He had seemed so angry, almost inappropriately so. So angry that she wondered if he'd ever be free of it, or its continuing crippling effects on his life.

Why she should doubt him or her perception of the man she thought she had come to know, she wasn't sure. Did she still question the veracity of his experiences, or was it something else altogether? Something more like an unsettled feeling? A discomfort even, with the barely contained and quite evidently unresolved resentment over the unfair way he had been treated since he had returned from the war? It festered in him like an infection that refused to heal. That he refused to allow to heal.

Sean struggled still with all that had happened to him. Struggled with God. Though his parents were godly people in every way, and eagerly resumed attending services at the Episcopal church in Grand View just as soon as Abby was finally able to tolerate the trip, Jessie had never seen Sean accompany them. That, combined with a few passing remarks he had made about the Lord, none of them complimentary, had only confirmed what she had feared all along. His angry bitterness had shut not only most people out of his heart but the Lord as well.

Her husband, Paul, had been estranged from God. That estrangement had been the one thing that had made her hesitate to wed him. She had been so young in those days, though, naively imagining her love would eventually turn him back to the Lord. But she wasn't so naive anymore. She didn't believe she could turn Sean back to God if he wasn't so inclined. From painful experience, she knew it'd take more than her love to induce a man to walk a higher, better path.

It was a hard reality to face, but face it this time she must. When it came to Sean MacKay, there were too many uncertainties. And it wasn't just about her own welfare and happiness anymore. She had to think of Emma.

The job offer in the Springs was concrete, certain. And Jessie was mightily weary of uncertainty and doubt. Yet why, even when she knew she was making the wisest, most logical move, did it hurt so badly to do so?

Though she hated to break such news the day before Christmas Eve, it was best if she began to sever the ties as soon as possible. She also needed time to ease the transition of Abby's care back to Conor and Claire. And, as for Sean, well, it wasn't as if she were moving all the way back to Baltimore. They could still see each other from time to time, continue trying to work things out. But only if he didn't take her departure the wrong way.

With a sad foreboding, Jessie pushed back her chair and rose. The sooner she told the MacKays of her decision, the sooner the pain would begin to ease. Some of the pain, but, she greatly feared, not all of it. Not all of it by a long shot.

Chapter Ten

"Conor, I'd like…a few minutes with our son," Abby said late the next morning, when he and Sean came to take her downstairs. "Privately, if you…don't mind."

Culdee Creek's owner sent Sean a questioning look but nodded his assent. "Sure. I'll be in the kitchen then, visiting with Jessie and Emma. Maybe I can even finagle a few Christmas cookies while I wait for Sean to fetch me when you're done."

His wife smiled. "You do that."

She waited until her husband had shut the door behind him, then turned to Sean, who had pulled up a chair by her bedside and taken a seat.

"Perhaps I was wrong to hope so, but I thought…there was something growing…between you and Jessie. Because of that, I hoped…that she wouldn't be so quick to take another job. Or, if she was offered one…you'd prevail upon her to turn it down and stay here."

Sean sighed and ran a hand through his hair. There were good and bad things about his mother's increasing ability to verbally communicate again. Most of which were good.

"Why do you immediately assume I had that kind of influence over her?" he asked. "She's been waiting for a paying job and finally got an offer. We all knew she'd up and leave just as soon as that happened."

Abby cocked her head and smiled. "I just had the impression… Well, perhaps I was wrong to assume certain things, to hope…"

You're not the only one who was beginning to hope, Sean silently replied. *But, evidently, I was mistaken.*

"Well," he forced himself to say instead, "whatever might have been growing between us got firmly quashed the other night when I finally told her what happened with Carl. She didn't waste much time yesterday, did she, informing us that she'd be moving on after Christmas. So, I say, good-bye and good riddance."

His mother laid a hand on his. "Don't be so quick…to write Jessie off, son. You can still visit her in the Springs. Maybe it's best…you let things slow down a bit. For both of your sakes…as well as for Emma's." She leaned back, releasing his hand. "Jessie told me her daughter had begged her…to let you be her new father."

Heat warmed Sean's cheeks. He hadn't known.

"That was probably the last straw for Jessie," he muttered. "A suspected coward and deserter as the father of her child."

"Do you really think she doesn't believe… your side of the story?"

"What does it matter? She expects me to forgive and forget." He gave a harsh laugh. "Well, hell will freeze over first."

"It's tearing you apart, son. Everyone who cares for you sees it. Even Jessie." She looked down. "And what possible good are you getting… from holding this anger and pain so close and for so long? Have you ever thought to ask yourself…what have you ever achieved in doing so? Compared to all that you've lost?"

What, indeed, had he achieved? Sean wondered. It hadn't brought back Carl or regained Charlotte's love. And, as far as Howard went, all his self-flagellation hadn't softened that man's heart, either. Atop it all, his unwillingness to forgive and put the past behind him might now also lose him Jessie just as, he realized with a sudden, sharp insight, it might well, in the end, have lost him Charlotte.

He shook his head and expelled a weary breath. "You're right, Ma. I can't say as I've gained anything, leastwise anything good. But I'm also not sure I deserve better than what I have, and got. It's just been so…so long now, I'm not sure I *can* be any different."

"You can if you finally find a way to forgive yourself…for whatever you imagine you did to contribute to all of this," his mother said. "The Lord surely forgave you a long time ago. So, how can you not do the same…when God, who is without sin, has forgiven your sins? Do any of us know better than He…what's forgivable and what isn't?"

"Ma," Sean said with a sigh. "You know how

I feel about God. Let's not get into another discussion about that."

"But it's part and parcel of the same issue, son. Are you yet so proud that you still believe that Jesus' sacrifice on the cross…was insufficient to permanently wash away all your sins…if only you repent of them and ask His forgiveness? Or are you the worst sinner of all in this world…and beyond even God's forgiveness? And is your pride turning you into a far, far greater fool…than some good, old-fashioned humility ever could?"

He stared at her, finally at a loss for words. What could he say at any rate? She knew he blamed God for what had happened. Blamed Him for Carl's untimely death, before he'd had a chance to grow up and redeem himself. For the loss of Charlotte's love and all those years of their failed, unhappy marriage. And for those precious babies of theirs who he'd never been able to hold, and teach, and love.

So much time lost, he thought, tears filling his eyes. *So much love denied. So much happiness squandered.*

His mother gazed at him, seeing, perceiving, understanding. "There's peace and enlightenment...to be found in every difficulty, Sean," she said softly. "Nothing good is ever lost. Everything—everything—is a gift from God...if only we accept and learn, grow, and never, ever, stop loving...or giving of ourselves."

"I know you believe that, Ma." He shoved back his chair and stood. "I know and am glad for you. I just don't see any gift in all of this. I'm sorry, but I just don't."

"But it's there nonetheless." Her eyes gleamed now with a fierce, joyous light. "It's there. You just have to want...to find and accept it. God's gift...and your gift back to God. The one perfect gift."

"Oh, look, Mama!" Emma danced around the parlor Christmas tree in delight early Christmas Eve. "Look at how many presents I have."

Jessie, who was sitting near the woodstove reading, glanced up and smiled at her daughter. "Yes, you do have a lot of presents, don't you? You'll have to be sure to thank the MacKays tomorrow morning for them."

"And Santa Claus too. Santa's coming tonight, you know, and he'll leave me presents too."

Besides the new pair of shoes—which had been labeled as a gift coming from Sean—that were under the tree, Jessie had added the stuffed Scotty dog and blue dress she had made. To top it off, besides a mysterious present from Abby and Conor—which from the looks of it she suspected might be a doll—Claire had also made her a dress, as well as a colorful lap quilt from her stash of feed-sack scraps. Jessie had saved the boxed puzzle and storybooks to put under the tree tonight from Santa. For a child who had received nothing last Christmas but a shiny red apple and a tattered storybook Jessie had been able to buy for five cents on a Baltimore street corner, tomorrow morning would seem like heaven.

"That's right, sweetheart." She exchanged a smiling look with Abby, who sat in the other wing chair, struggling with the scarf she was attempting to crochet. The craft was but another way to exercise her weak hand, not to mention it provided the older woman with a task that made her once again feel useful. "Santa's coming tonight."

"As is the Christ child," Abby added. "Most importantly of all, this is the night of the Baby Jesus' birth." She glanced at Jessie. "Maybe your mama would like to read us the story from the Bible."

"Oh yes, Mama!" Emma clapped her hands and jumped up and down. "We can't forget to read the Christmas story, can we?"

"No, we certainly can't." Jessie rose. "I'll just be a minute, while I go up to our room and fetch—"

"That won't be necessary." Abby pointed to the glass-fronted bookcase. "The MacKay family Bible is in there. You can use it."

As Jessie headed to the bookcase, the front door opened, bringing with it a blast of cold air. Two pairs of booted feet, stomping off snow, were next heard in the foyer. She opened the bookcase door, pulled out the huge old Bible, and turned.

There stood Conor and Sean. They had given all the ranch hands today and tomorrow off and had just finished putting up the livestock for the evening. Their expressions, however, were hardly those of men who had done a hard day's work and were now relieved to be finished.

"There's some sort of fire at the Rowles's farm," Conor said. "From the size of it, appears like it might be their barn."

Abby laid down her crocheting. "Oh, my. Their house isn't all that far from their barn. What if—"

"I know." Her husband cut her off. "I'm going to fetch Evan, then head over and see if they can use some help." He turned to Sean. "Seeing as how our ranch hands are gone, the Rowleses might could use any and all help. Care to join us?"

Jessie watched Sean's expression go taut. His shuttered glance met hers. She knew what his answer would be even before he replied.

"I hardly think Howard will want my help," he growled, looking away. "Knowing that proud old coot, he'd rather lose his barn and house before letting me put one foot on his place."

"Nevertheless, it's the decent thing to do, son. And you're a decent man."

"Howard Rowles wouldn't recognize decent if it stared him in the face!"

Culdee Creek's owner sighed and grasped his son by the shoulder. "Don't you think it's past time you stop letting other folks' expectations of you determine your actions? Do what's in your heart, son, and you'll never go wrong."

For a long moment, Sean didn't reply. Watching the emotions that played across his face, Jessie held her breath. *Please, Lord*, she prayed. *Let him be the man I hoped he was. Let him do what's in his heart, and let that heart be good and honorable.*

Once more, their gazes met and, as he stared at her, something changed, softened. He expelled a deep breath, then nodded.

"Fine," he muttered, looking to his father. "I'll go. I'll offer him my help. But mark my words. He won't take it."

"Tonight of all nights, maybe he will, son," his father softly replied. "Tonight's a night of miracles, after all. The night of greatest miracles and perfect gifts."

"I'll go too," Jessie said, determined not only to lend a hand but also to support Sean in what might still be a difficult undertaking. Both men turned to her in surprise. "And why not? If I can't help with hauling water, I'm sure Mrs. Rowles could use me in some other capacity."

"Yes," Abby piped up just then. "You all go.

Emma will be fine here with me. We'll read the Christmas story together…then play games and eat cookies and drink up all the eggnog."

"Well, okay then." Conor looked to Jessie. "We need to get going soon, though."

"Give me five minutes to change into jeans, boots, and a shirt," she said. "You'll need at least that much time to get the truck out and call Evan, at any rate."

"You're right." He glanced at Sean. "Why don't you get the truck, load up as many buckets as you can find, while I call Evan. And you, missy," he added, turning back to Jessie, "head upstairs and get changed. And dress warm, in layers. It's going to be one cold and probably very wet night."

The expression on Howard Rowles's soot-blackened face when he saw Sean climb out of the truck and begin handing buckets to his father and brother said it all. As he approached them like some bulldog spoiling for a fight, Sean set down the last of the buckets, squared his shoulders, and awaited the older man's arrival.

"Thanks for coming, MacKay," Rowles said,

offering his hand to Conor while pointedly ignoring Sean at least for the moment. "We can use all the help we can get. The barn's a goner, but the wind's picked up and it's going to be tight if we're to save the house."

"We're neighbors, Howard," Conor replied, taking his hand. "Always were and always will be. And neighbors help neighbors in times like these."

"I'm obliged." The other man finally looked at Sean. "I'll take your help, and that of Evan. And even that of Mrs. Ashmore. But I can't accept Sean's. I just can't."

"You need every able body you can get, Rowles," Sean growled. "Unless you want to risk losing your home."

"I'd rather lose even that than ever be beholden to your sort, MacKay," Howard snarled. "Nothing you can ever do will ingratiate yourself back into my good graces. Nothing!"

Sean's laugh was harsh, brittle. "I'm not doing this for you, Rowles. I'm doing this for myself." A sudden surety filled him, and with it came a bittersweet sense of finality and peace. "It doesn't matter anymore if you ever forgive me. But I'm bound and determined to forgive myself. I've paid my fair share and more for what happened to Carl. I'm done paying."

"Get out of here!" Howard shouted. "Get off my place before I throw you off. You're a sniveling coward and—"

"Enough, Howard. We've got a house to save." From out of the darkness, Mary Rowles strode up to stand beside her husband. "It's past time I told you the truth, and the truth is, it's never been Sean's fault. Not any of it."

He angled back from her, his eyes widening in surprise. "What are you talking about, woman?"

She bit her lip, sent Sean a shamefaced look. "I was wrong to keep this secret for so long," she said, meeting him eye to eye for the first time in years. "I chose my husband over what was right and true. Someday, I hope you'll forgive me."

Then she riveted her gaze back on her husband. "There was a second letter. One Carl wrote the day he died. In it, he finally confessed that he had lied about Sean in that first letter we got. It had all been Carl's fault. He was the one who deserted. He just tried to blame Sean because Sean's record was spotless, and his wasn't. He thought both of them, that way, would escape the firing squad and just be court-martialed. But he was wrong, and he died for it."

Sean watched the blood drain from Howard's face. "A—a second letter? I never saw any second letter."

"We didn't get it until after the army notified us of Carl's death," his wife said. "And you were so devastated that I didn't see the harm in keeping it from you. I thought…I thought I could at least spare you the added pain of knowing"—she paused, swallowed hard, then continued—"that it was your son who was the deserter and coward."

"No!" Tears filled Rowles's eyes and coursed down his cheeks. "No, I don't believe it."

To her credit, this time Mary didn't back down. "I still have the letter. And I'll show it to you, but not right now. Right now, we've got a fire to fight. And we need the help of all three of these fine MacKay men."

When Howard just stood there, staring dumbfounded down at his wife, Sean decided he'd had enough. Though Mary Rowles's revelation was a belated godsend, he was bemused to find that it was also anticlimactic. The instant he had made the decision to forgive himself, the ponderous weight on his heart had lifted. It was as if someone had lifted the burden from him. Someone…God.

"Here." He stooped, picked up two buckets, and handed them to his brother. Then, two more, and handed them to his father. The last two, he picked up himself. "We don't have any more time to waste. Let's go fight a fire."

Howard Rowles lifted his head, shot him an agonized look. A look of confusion mixed with entreaty. An entreaty for forgiveness.

Sean nodded in reply, then stepped out, heading toward the fire.

Chapter Eleven

Damp, blackened from head to toe, and numb from the cold, they arrived home around eleven that night. After carrying Emma, who had fallen asleep on the sofa, upstairs and tucking her in, Jessie was still too restless and unsettled to take to her own bed. Changing into dry clothes, she headed downstairs to the kitchen, intent on making herself a soothing cup of chamomile tea. The fire in Old Bess had yet to be banked, so the addition of several sticks of wood soon had it burning hotly again.

The house was quiet, Conor and Sean having evidently helped Abby up to her bed, then settled in themselves for the night. The kitchen was warm and cozy after the hours spent in the freezing weather, battered by the wind and soaked with the countless buckets of water hauled in the process of finally putting out the fire. The barn had been a total loss, but the Rowles's farmhouse was safe and sound.

The kettle whistled at long last, and Jessie made her tea. Clasping the pottery mug to her, she stood there for a time at the kitchen window, inhaling deeply of the pleasing, flowerlike scent. Eventually, though, she stirred in two teaspoons of honey, then took her seat at the table.

A lot had changed tonight, she thought, sipping carefully of the hot, fragrant brew. Sean had finally broken through the barriers he had so solidly built about his heart for so many years. He had not only forgiven himself, but Howard—and Mary—Rowles as well. It would likely take some time for them all to feel comfortable with each other again, to talk out all the pain and hostility they had harbored for so long, but at least it was a beginning.

She was happy for Sean, on so many levels. He was indeed the good, courageous, honorable man she had come to imagine he was, before the incident with Howard Rowles in Gates Mercantile. Indeed, his fortitude in finally moving past his anger and unwillingness to forgive put her own weaknesses to shame.

"Help me, Lord," she whispered, lowering her head, "to be as brave and generous as Sean. To forgive, once and for all, Paul's failings. To look with compassion, and not with anger, at Louise's lifelong inability to give or receive love, save for what little she was finally able to muster for her granddaughter. And to forgive myself for anything I may have done to disappoint Paul or hurt Louise."

Her hands still clasped about her mug, Jessie prayed for a time. Gradually she felt the old, all too familiar tensions ease. She smiled. *I have so little to give You, Lord, on this night of miracles, the eve of Your birth*, she thought, *but all I have, I offer. My one perfect gift...a humble, contrite, loving heart.*

Footsteps echoed down the hallway toward the kitchen. Jessie quickly swiped away the tears that had filled her eyes. She turned in her chair to face the door just as Sean walked in.

For an instant he stood there, apparently

startled to see her. He had washed up, his face now free of soot, his dark hair combed back from his forehead and, though he wore a clean shirt and jeans, he was barefoot. It brought to mind another late night in the kitchen, when she had inadvertently come upon him fresh from his bath. At the memory, Jessie blushed.

"I didn't expect anyone to still be awake," he said, echoing similar words he had spoken that other night.

"I didn't, either." She smiled and gestured to the kettle. "The water's still hot if you'd like to make yourself some tea."

He hesitated for so long that Jessie thought he had either come to the kitchen for some other reason altogether or just plain didn't want to be around her. Which was understandable. He had been far from happy when she'd told him of her plans to accept the job at Bethel General Hospital. She wished now she hadn't so quickly taken the job, or at least had waited a while to tell him. If she had, she might have avoided the rift that had since formed between them.

"Sure." Sean walked to the cupboard and took out a mug, then a tea bag from a covered bowl.

"I'm too wound up to sleep just yet." He grinned. "Fighting fires in the freezing cold tends to do that to a man."

"And to a woman." Jessie let out a breath, surprised to discover she'd been holding it.

He filled his mug with steaming water from the stove, then added the tea bag. Pulling out a chair, Sean sat and began to dunk the tea bag in and out of his water.

She watched him for a time, forming and reforming what she knew she needed to say. Finally, with a frustrated sigh, Jessie just let the words come.

"I was wrong about you. I realized that tonight. I hope you'll accept my apology."

"Apology accepted," he said, meeting her gaze. "Not that you *were* wrong about me *until* tonight. It just all finally came together, what you'd said, what my family had been saying to me all along." His mouth lifted in a sheepish grin. "Never let it be said that I'm a fast learner, or long on humility."

"It's hard to forgive when someone causes you pain or great disappointment." Jessie paused to take a sip of her tea. "I haven't been overly kind or forgiving of some people in my life, either.

But, thanks to your example, I'm going to. Your example and the good Lord's help."

"Yeah, the good Lord." He looked down. "I'm thinking it's past time I ask for more of that help too. I don't think I could've done what I did tonight without it."

Like a rose opening its petals to the warmth of the sun, happiness unfolded in Jessie's heart. Thanks to her impulse to run away when things got tough, she may well have lost her chance with Sean. But at least she'd leave knowing that, someday, he might again open his heart to love. That knowledge wasn't all that she would've desired, but it had to be enough.

"I'm glad to hear that. It'll make leaving here all that much easier."

His eyes narrowed. He leaned forward. "Why, Jessie? Why will knowing I'm giving my life back over to God make it easier for you to leave?"

Sudden, hot tears flooded her eyes. She looked away. "Why? Because…because as hard as you might find this to believe, I still care about what happens to you. I wasn't just wrong about you. I was wrong to…" She shook her head, wiped away her tears. "Well, it doesn't matter. What's done is done, and likely for the best."

He didn't say anything, just stared so hard at her she thought his gaze would pierce clear through her. Or at least to the depths of her heart, where he'd finally see the truth.

"You don't have to take that job, Jessie," Sean said softly at last. "My mother can still use your help. You—and Emma—can stay right where you are."

Was there a deeper meaning beneath his words, Jessie wondered, or was he just being kind, or practical, or a combination of both?

"These days, hospital jobs don't come around all that often." Her gaze dropped to her mug. "And your mother won't need me much longer. In fact, she doesn't even need the services of a nurse anymore."

"Then what about me? Am I as easy to walk away from as it seems my mother is?"

Eyes wide, Jessie looked up. "Is that what I've led all of you to think? That I haven't come to care—and care deeply—for all of you? That your home's nothing but a place to fill my belly and lay my head? Well, that couldn't be further from the truth. And *you're* especially not easy to walk away from, Sean. Far, far from it."

An emotion—was it hope, joy?—flared in his eyes. He reached over, took her hand. "Then don't go, Jessie. Stay. Stay for my mother. Stay"—his voice broke—"stay for me."

Her own throat clogged with freshened tears, but she forced the words past nonetheless. "Why? Why do you want me to stay?"

For an instant, she saw hesitation flicker in his eyes and feared he'd draw back, not utter what she so longed to hear. Then he dragged in a deep, steadying breath.

"Why else? Why else but that I love you, Jessie. Love you and want you to be my wife."

Though she knew they both needed more time to sort everything out, to get to know each other better, his words filled her with such joy. And it was a start. A very, very promising start.

"So am I to take that as a proposal of marriage then?" she asked with a smile. "Because, if it is, I accept. We'll need a bit longer engagement period, though. Two months, even for two people who've both been married, is a bit short, don't you think?"

He shrugged. "I suppose so. How does Valentine's Day sound for a wedding then?"

She cocked her head, pretending to appear doubtful. "Two months from now? Well, that would make it almost four months since we first met. Sounds like a reasonable amount of time to me."

"More than reasonable," Sean said, getting up from the table to come around, pull her to her feet, and take her into his arms. "I mean, from what I heard, Emma apparently decided a while ago that she wanted me as her father."

Jessie laughed. "Well, they always say children are much quicker to figure things out than adults."

"Then we should have plenty of them, don't you think, to help us figure things out?"

In the parlor, the mantel clock began to chime, signaling it was finally midnight. Midnight, the moment of Christ's birth, Jessie thought. On a Christmas Eve that she'd long remember as one of the happiest ones of her life.

Standing on tiptoe, she kissed Sean full on the lips. "Yes, we should plan on having plenty of children," she whispered. "I've always had a particular fondness for that verse from Genesis, you know."

He frowned, puzzled. "And exactly which one would that be?"

"What else?" Jessie asked with a joyous giggle. "Be fruitful, and multiply, and replenish the earth!"

About the Author

Kathleen Morgan is the author of the Brides of
Culdee Creek Series as well as the These Highland
Hills Series. She lives in Colorado.

Kathleen loves to hear from her readers. You
can contact her at www.kathleenmorgan.com.

Love Inspired®
SUSPENSE
RIVETING INSPIRATIONAL ROMANCE

These contemporary tales
of intrigue and romance
feature Christian characters
facing challenges to their faith...
and their lives!

**Four new Love Inspired Suspense titles are
available every month wherever books are
sold, including most bookstores, supermarkets,
drug stores and discount stores.**

Steeple
Hill®

Visit:
www.steeplehillbooks.com